THE MUFFIN CHILD

THE
MUFFIN CHILD

STEPHEN MENICK

PHILOMEL BOOKS • NEW YORK

Patricia Lee Gauch, editor

Text copyright © 1998 by Stephen Menick. All rights reserved.
This book, or parts thereof, may not be reproduced
in any form without permission in writing from the publisher,
Philomel Books, a division of Penguin Putnam Books for Young Readers,
345 Hudson Street, New York, NY 10014.
Philomel, Reg. U.S. Pat. & Tm. Off.
Published simultaneously in Canada. Printed in the United States.
Book design by Gunta Alexander. Text set in Arrus

Library of Congress Cataloging-in-Publication Data
Menick, Stephen. The muffin child / Stephen Menick. p. cm.
Summary: When her parents die in an accident in 1913,
eleven-year-old Tanya decides to live alone, refusing charity from
the people in her village, and supporting herself by selling muffins.
[1. Orphans—Fiction. 2. Death—Fiction. 3. Resourcefulness—Fiction.]
I. Title PZ7.M5275Mu 1998 [Fic]—dc21 97-51817 CIP AC
ISBN 0-399-23303-2
1 3 5 7 9 10 8 6 4 2
First Impression

In memory of my mother

THE MUFFIN CHILD

CHAPTER
ONE

If you're not going to lis-
ten," her mother said, "I'm not going to read to you."

There it was again, the little wrinkle when her
mother's mouth went tense: the half circle around the
corner of her mouth, like a fingernail paring, or the
moon at its thinnest in the sky.

"Tanya?" her mother said. "You're not listening."

"I am too listening."

Her mother closed the book.

"What if I told you a story?"

"You are telling me a story," Tanya said, fed up with
her mother's stories that made no sense, and not want-
ing to give an inch.

"I mean really told you a story. Not out of a book.
Would you like me to tell it to you?"

"If you want."

"No, I want you to tell me you're going to listen to the story," her mother said. "To every word of it."

"All right, I'll listen."

"It's about a girl like you."

"Are you making this up?"

"It's about a girl who lost her father."

Tanya didn't say anything.

"And not only her father," her mother went on. "She lost her mother too. It happened a long time ago. It happened in 1913. But that doesn't make it any different. The girl was your age. So when I tell you the story, I want you to put your own face on her. Make believe she's you. Will you do that?"

Tanya shrugged.

"First I have to tell you about the country she lived in. Are you listening?"

CHAPTER
TWO

It was an old country in the Balkans, a puzzle of hills and valleys, and the streams turned the water mills to grind the farmers' wheat. In the dark little churches the candlelight licked the silver frames on the pictures of bearded saints. There were villages where the people crossed themselves when they prayed, and villages where they bowed down on red rugs and prayed to God under the minarets. It was the kind of country where nothing much ever changes, where the past never dies, and the present never forgets.

One railroad ran through the land, but Tanya had never seen it. She lived in a stone house, with a thatch roof like a haystack. Beside the house stood the barn, and it, too, was made of stone and thatch. By the house and barn was a dirt road, then a river gorge, and a village across the river. The river moved swiftly, fed by the clouds that gathered over the mountains.

A raincloud rolled over the village one afternoon in the fall, at the end of market day; Tanya had spent the day with her parents in the village square, selling things from the farm. The rain turned the day into night, and everyone hurried to close up. Tanya helped her parents load the wagon. She had an armful of apples, and they tumbled from her arm. They bounced on the wet cobblestones, and she ran to pick them up, and then they all climbed into the wagon and drove through the streets. The rain streamed off the tiled roofs of the houses, pounding like fists on the roof of the wagon.

The river was high. Tanya saw foam when they came to the old stone bridge. The horse didn't want to cross. Her father snapped the reins and the horse moved forward. The river hardly fit under the bridge. Tanya was sitting between her parents, and she shut her eyes in fright as the great branch of a tree reached out in front of them and barred the way. She felt a thump. The bridge shook.

Because her eyes were shut, she couldn't see Milenka, their cow, standing in the road on the other side of the bridge. Whenever the family went to the village market, it was always Tanya's job to close the barn door, but sometimes she forgot and the cow would wander out, and Tanya's father would become cross with her. It had happened again. Her father shouted at her.

"How many times have I told you to bolt that door! Run ahead and put Milenka inside! Run!"

"Be careful, Tanya!" her mother called after her. Tanya jumped down from the wagon. Suddenly her shoes were soaking wet, her feet ice-cold. She ducked under the branch, ran across the bridge, and pushed the cow with both hands. The river roared behind her. She would always remember those two things together because they both happened at once: the roar of the river in her ears and the feel of Milenka's wet hide against the palms of her hands. She turned and saw the river looking like a hump of white water over a stone in a mountain stream, but big, bigger than the bridge, and she couldn't see the bridge anymore.

CHAPTER
THREE

Some things you never think about, not because they can't happen, but because you wouldn't know what to do if they ever happened.

Tanya's parents had never said to her: "When we die . . . " or: "If anything ever happens to us . . . " She'd never imagined that her parents wouldn't always be near her. So when she pushed the cow in the rain and turned around and didn't see them anywhere, she didn't believe it.

She didn't see the bridge break and crumble into the river or the wagon wheels upturned and drowning in the foam. She knew that the wagon had been stuck on the bridge with the tree barring the way, and that the bridge, the tree and the wagon were gone. But there was no place in her mind for the thought that she could lose her parents—no place at all, except in that shadowy world where the impossible happened while she slept.

But dreams were things you woke up from; and Tanya wanted this so badly to be a dream, she woke up the next morning thinking her parents would come back. They weren't gone forever. They would come back. And it was this way she found of surviving the loss of her parents that set her life on its new course, and would send her to places she never knew existed.

In the morning a voice that sounded like her mother's called from downstairs.

"Tanya? Tanya!"

A man's voice called. It sounded like her father. "Tanya!"

Footsteps climbed the wooden stairs, and a woman and a man appeared. They were Mother Anna and her husband Pavel, from the village across the river, leaning under the rafters of Tanya's room.

"The poor thing, in bed in her wet clothes!"

The day was dim and gray with fog, but the fog outside wasn't as thick as the one within Tanya, the one that made the day seem unreal to her. She could hear people's voices, but everyone seemed far away.

"Pavel, build a fire in the hearth and heat water for a bath. Hurry."

When the water was ready, Mother Anna carried Tanya downstairs to the kitchen and gave her a bath in a big copper basin in front of the hearth. Tanya felt the warmth of the fire and the warm water trickling down her back when Mother Anna squeezed the sponge, but that too seemed far away, as though it were happening to someone else. Mother Anna poured another pot of water into the basin, and the waterfall frightened Tanya.

"It's all right, dear," Mother Anna said.

Tanya sat in dry clothes by the hearth, gazing into the flames. Other people from the village were in the barnyard, talking about the fallen bridge and about her mother and father. She heard the words, "washed into the sea."

She ran from the house and opened the barn door.

Milenka was there, where Tanya had put her last night, knowing that when her parents came home, they would want exactly that.

The spotted cow turned her head as Tanya came running in. Tanya threw her arms around Milenka's neck.

"Did you catch a cold?" Tanya said, stroking Milenka. "I'm sorry I left the door open. I'm sorry I didn't milk you this morning. I forgot. I'll do it right now."

She felt a man's arms taking her gently. It was Pavel.

"Milenka's fine, Tanya," he said. "I already milked her. Come back into the house."

Then she was sitting in front of the hearth again, holding a cup of Milenka's milk in her hands.

"Listen to me, dear," Mother Anna said. "Don't you hear me? Drink some milk, and then we'll get your things together and take you home with us."

Just then—when Mother Anna said, "take you home with us"—just then Tanya seemed to come out of her daze a little. She smelled the fire. It was applewood burning.

"My mother and father are coming home soon," she said, and took a long gulp of milk.

"Of course they are, dear, but you can't wait here all by yourself. You need someone to take care of you in the meantime."

"They're coming home soon and I have to be here for them when they come."

"Of course, dear."

Tanya was staring at the fire, at the sparks flying up into the chimney. Her mother had once told her that the sparks from a fire were souls going to heaven. They flew so fast, they were gone in an instant.

"We won't talk about it anymore now," Mother Anna said.

They left the house. Mother Anna held Tanya's hand. The hills rose steep and dark on either side, and the evening light skipped over the river and painted it pink. They came to what was left of the bridge, stone stumps on either side of the gorge. The masts of two cypresses had been laid across, and hammers had been busy all day. There were planks and wooden railings now, so people could cross again. Tanya didn't want to go. Pavel picked her up and carried her.

She was hardly thinking at all, but as Pavel carried her into the village, she thought of something that happened every year in the villages in those hills. It was called the procession of Saint Marissa. Once a year in the spring, on Saint Marissa's eve, the people would gather and walk with candles down to the river, and set the candles adrift, floating in little paper boats. The flickering boats would slip away and everyone would stand at the river's edge and watch them go. It was a strange, impressive thing to be a part of, or even just to watch. Strangest of all was the picture of Saint Marissa, which the oldest man, walking in front, would cradle in his arms so that everyone could see it. The picture was a holy thing. People were almost afraid of it. They would stop whatever they were doing and stare at it in silence. They did the same with Tanya as she was carried through the streets of the village.

She didn't feel holy. She felt almost guilty. She saw the faces in the windows, and the faces were all looking at her, and no one spoke. "Why are they looking at me?" she wondered. "What have I done?"

Pavel and Mother Anna brought Tanya to their house, into the kitchen. Their children were waiting, and the fire was snapping in the hearth. Strings of red peppers hung to dry like a hundred red rags on clotheslines. Pavel put Tanya on a bench beside the hearth, under the red peppers. Tanya sat holding her knees. Mother Anna made supper. The children already knew what had happened. They didn't come near Tanya, but stared at her as if she were about to be punished for something and the punishment frightened them. The youngest child squeaked: "Why is everybody so quiet? What's the matter with Tanya?"

There was another child, and he was the only one who didn't stare. Nikola didn't look at Tanya at all. He was busy playing with his blocks. Nikola was seven, too big to be playing with blocks. But Nikola was different from other boys. He could hear, but he never said a word. He lived in a world of his own, apart from everyone and everything except his blocks. They were alphabet blocks, and were so worn down they were almost round. Nikola was never without his blocks, and he would spend hours putting one on top of the other, turning them different ways, just as he was doing now. He sat in front of the hearth, on the floor where the flagstones toasted in the heat, the blocks going click clack, click clack.

Nikola didn't sleep with his brothers and sisters in the other room because he would waken them in the middle of the night with the click clack of his blocks. He slept upstairs in a room under the roof, a little space he shared with chests and trunks, a birdcage and a broken rocking horse. Tonight he shared it with Tanya, too. Mother Anna held a lamp while Pavel unrolled a mattress, and then she passed the lamp to Pavel and got sheets and a blanket and made Tanya's new bed, shaking a plump pillow into a pillowcase. Tanya was still in her fog. She let herself be undressed and helped into her own nightshirt, which Mother Anna had brought from across the river.

Mother Anna tucked her in, but too tight, and Tanya couldn't move. She didn't kick and punch her way free just yet, but she waited until Mother Anna and Pavel were gone. They stood for a moment in the hall at the bottom of the steps. The lamp in Pavel's hand swayed a little as it shined up the steps, and the shadow of the rocking horse stretched its neck over the rafters.

"Can we afford another child?" Pavel said.

"What else can we do?" Mother Anna said.

CHAPTER
FOUR

Tanya had no other family, no aunts or uncles or grandparents in the village or even in the hills nearby. Her mother and father had crossed the mountains when Tanya was a baby, after her father's uncle died and passed the farm on to him. The uncle's wife, Tanya's great-aunt, had lived with them until Tanya was five; and Tanya was the only child.

She wasn't used to sleeping with another child in the room, or going to bed in any house but the one she knew. She heard Nikola breathing through his mouth, heard the other children turning in their bed in the other room; and in the deep quiet she heard the plop of a log settling in the ashes in the hearth downstairs. The sound of a hearth was the sound of home, the same everywhere. But here the sound seemed to change on its way upstairs. This house sounded different, felt different. It wasn't her house, and this wasn't her family. Click clack.

Click. She heard it and didn't know what it was at first. The world was dark and she didn't know where she was in it. The covers were loose but she was afraid to move. Clack. She remembered Nikola. She remembered where she was, and then she began to remember why. Some terrible thing had happened, and she could feel it pushing into her thoughts, pressing her down into a darkness deeper than the one that surrounded her. And the only way to keep from sinking deeper was to remember that her parents were on their way home.

She sat up and gasped for air. She was in Nikola's room, Nikola was playing with his blocks, and it was still night. There was still time.

There was a shade of blue in the window, the first hint of morning, and Tanya knew she had to hurry. She pulled her nightshirt off and got into her cotton teddy and sweater and skirt. Nikola was up, rolling his blocks like wheels. Tanya put her socks on but not her shoes, not just yet. She stuffed her nightshirt under her arm and, holding her shoes, went carefully down the first steps to the hall.

If it had been her own house, she wouldn't have had to use her toes as feelers and find where the steps ended, going down one foot at a time. In her own house her feet knew every inch of every step and every bump and dimple in the floor. But here, she couldn't remember where the walls opened up to become doors or where the floor dropped out to become stairs. With one hand she felt along the wall (she heard Mother Anna snoring and the clock ticking on the night table in another room) and she stuck her toes out to check the floor until she came to the top of the stairs. She sat at the top of the stairs, put her nightshirt and shoes in her lap, and went down sitting all the way.

It didn't take long. When her toes touched the stone floor of the kitchen and she could make out the pale cracks in the shutters, she put her shoes on. She could tie her shoes perfectly well in the dark.

A mouse scrabbled in a corner. The hearth smelled of ashes, like stale pepper. In the middle of the kitchen Tanya banged into a chair. She froze, waiting to hear if she'd woken anyone. Upstairs, Pavel muttered something. Tanya eased the latch to the door and slipped out.

The street was paved with cobblestones, bumpy, like corn on the cob, with a gutter running down the middle. The stones were slick with dew. Tanya knew her way. She hurried down the street, down another and another narrow way where the stone walls of the houses were so close, you could lean out the window and hand a plate to your neighbor. She crossed the village square, empty at this hour. The square sloped down into a long street to the bridge. From an alley came the splash of a bucket of water. A white cat looked over its shoulder at

Tanya and skittered away, the only white thing among the deep blues and grays of early morning.

Across the planks of the bridge she went, those fresh white planks that weren't there two nights ago; she went quickly over the whispering river. She looked far down the road, thinking she might see her parents coming. She had heard of dogs and cats and horses falling into the river and swept along and thought lost for sure, and then someone found them, wet and cold but safe. If animals could save themselves, why not her parents, who were so much smarter?

Her parents were young and strong, and people who were young and strong weren't the dying kind. Tanya had never said this to herself, but she believed it with all her heart, because it was what her life had taught her. She knew that babies could die because they were tiny and weak, and she knew that people died when they got old. Tanya's great-aunt, the one who had lived with them in the house, had died because she was old.

That was what Tanya's mother had told her: that Baba died of old age and God had wanted her to rest. Tanya remembered the priest with the long black beard and the black stovepipe hat who came to the house after Baba took to her bed. The priest chanted in deep tones and swung a smoking brass vessel with the smoke that smelled wonderful, and then Baba wasn't there anymore. No one smiled for a few days, but it was spring and the smiles did come back, and the hillsides turned a soft green almost overnight and it was all part of the order of things, the way things were. Tanya could understand that. But that had nothing to do with her parents.

She came home. She passed through the gate into the barnyard. There were no animals out. Nothing had changed. She entered the house.

"Momma? Papa?"

The kitchen was dark, and the ashes in the hearth were cold. Her parents were so tired after their ordeal, they had gone straight to bed the moment they got back. Tanya pounded up the stairs to their room. She hoped they hadn't been worried when they found the house without her in it. They must have known she was in the village, at Mother Anna and Pavel's.

As the door to her parents' room swung back, it banged against the wardrobe behind it. The curtains were drawn and Tanya couldn't see the bed.

"Momma?"

In the bed were two valleys, like the ruts in the road from the wagon wheels. The valley on one side was her father's, the valley on the other side was her mother's place. Tanya felt the valleys. They were empty.

She flopped down hard, across the two valleys, and the bed creaked the way it creaked when her parents climbed into bed at night.

This was the sound she used to hear from her own bed in the next room—the sound that meant that her parents were finding rest and comfort at the end of their long day, and were about to go gratefully to sleep. Tanya wanted to hear that sound again. She wanted everyone home and in bed. Lying now on her parents' bed, she pushed down and jiggled to make it creak.

The bump between the valleys in the bed pressed against her stomach. She lay there, trying to dream the silence of the house away—trying to fill the silence with imagined footsteps, the rattle of the latch of the front door, her mother's voice calling her.

Then she thought of Milenka. She should milk Milenka. Tanya went out and crossed the barnyard. The dawn was turning purple, with the sliver of the moon like a golden weather vane on top of the barn.

It was warm inside the barn and it had that smell Tanya loved, the smell of cow and hay. The chickens rustled in their coop, and the geese in their pen lifted their heads and looked. Tanya heard something up in the hayloft—the barn owl, home after a night's work.

"Good morning, Milenka," Tanya said, and as Milenka turned her head, Tanya felt the cow's warm, wet breath on her arms. She reached down and pulled, and Milenka's milk squirted into the pail and smelled sweet.

Tanya did her morning chores, as she would do every day because her parents expected it. She cleaned the coops. The geese were out squawking in the barnyard when she came back into the house with milk and eggs and butter ready to be churned. She got busy working the butter churn. Then she took a moment to rest, and thought of the muffins she wouldn't have this morning, because her mother wasn't there to make them for her.

But it was still early. Maybe they were coming right now, coming up the road. Tanya went outside, out through the gate, and looked down the river. A man from the village was slowly leading a mule and a cart across the bridge, testing the new planks. They held, and he turned to go down the road. She didn't know who he was—he was too far away—but she liked him. He was a friend, a neighbor, a good man. Surely he would meet her parents on the road, give them a ride, and they would all come up to the house together.

Telling herself to be patient, she went back indoors. The kitchen was a gloomy place. She built a fire in the hearth.

Everything Tanya needed for the fire was there in the kitchen. There were dried leaves in a basket, twigs, and logs. She took some leaves and sprinkled them on the ashes in the hearth. Over the leaves she built a house of twigs. She took a log from the stack, and thought of her father working for hours, chopping wood. She passed her hand along the flesh of the wood before laying it on the fiery twigs.

She was basking in the heat when the thought came to her to warm up the oven and make muffins for her parents. They would be hungry when they came. They would welcome a plate of hot muffins waiting for them. They would all have muffins and tea—Tanya, her parents, and that man driving the cart.

As she sat now by the hearth, she could see them around the table with herself in the picture, and she could see the hands taking the muffins from the plate until the last muffin was gone. She could see the yellow plate with its garland of painted apples and its bumps, going round and round, from the potter's fingers. It was one of her mother's plates in the cupboard. Then Tanya remembered she didn't know how to make muffins. She didn't know her mother's recipe. The picture faded from her mind.

A moment later, it came back. Like a visitor knocking on a door, knocking a second time, the picture came back. She could fill that plate. She'd watched her mother do it many times.

Tanya went to the cupboard and took down one of the plates. It was heavy as stone. She laid it on the table and tried to see muffins there. She was afraid in a way that she couldn't explain to herself, but she went ahead anyway.

First she had to build a fire in the firebox in the oven. She got the fire going with a burning twig from the hearth. Then she closed the firebox door and opened the vent so the flames could breathe. The flames glowed through the vent and hummed as the air rushed in.

By the time she finished churning the butter, the oven was almost hot enough. She beat two eggs and mixed in the butter and some of Milenka's milk. She scooped flour from her mother's jar. Next came sugar, baking powder and a little salt.

The oven and the fire in the hearth warmed the kitchen. The morning sunlight in the window warmed Tanya's face, and the swirl of flour glittered in the air. Somehow Tanya felt close to her mother, as though her mother were beside her, helping her. The batter seemed too thick, and Tanya heard her mother say: "Tanya, it needs more milk." She poured some more milk. "Not too much!" her mother whispered. Tanya stirred the batter until it was smooth. She paused to wonder if she'd forgotten anything—spice! Her mother had many spices, red and yellow powders, green and black leaves, all in little glass jars. Tanya couldn't remember which of the spices was for muffins. She chose an orange powder because she liked its smell. The batter was ready.

Into the oven went the muffin pan, and soon the smell filled the kitchen. Tanya could hardly sit still. She kept peeking into the oven. She filled the tea kettle and got it started on the flame. Out came the muffins when they were golden and fluffy, the way her mother made them. Tanya tipped the pan over and put the six steaming muffins on a plate. She knew they were still too hot to eat. She knew she should wait for her parents. But she had to taste one. She took a muffin between her thumb and middle finger, and she was about to bite into it when the latch turned in the door. It was her parents. They were right on time.

"There you are! You had us scared to death!"

Mother Anna barged in, with Nikola in her arms and Pavel behind her. Tanya put the muffin down.

"We've been looking everywhere for you!" Mother Anna said. "We were afraid you—why did you sneak out of the house like that?"

"I came home," Tanya said.

Mother Anna's eyes went to the muffins on the plate. "Where did you get those muffins?"

"I made them."

Nikola was squirming in Mother Anna's arms. She put him in a chair by the table. He played with his blocks, click clack, click clack on the table. In came two other couples from the village.

"It's all right, we found her," Pavel said to them. "She's here."

Now the kitchen was full of people and noise. There were six grownups, all talking about Tanya and how she'd had them so worried. Mother Anna turned to her and said:

"Dear heart! You can't just leave the house in the middle of the night without telling anyone! If you're going to be part of our household, you've got to live by our rules, dear. I don't know how your parents raised you—"

"They're coming back today," Tanya said.

In the silence, Nikola banged his blocks together. Then the tea kettle started whistling.

"Tea!" Pavel said, smacking his hands together. "Let's have tea!" He lifted the kettle from the fire. "Tanya, where'd your mother keep the tea leaves? Can I try one of your muffins?"

He helped himself to one.

"What are you looking at me for?" Pavel said to Mother Anna with his mouth full. "Let's relax and have breakfast. She's fine. False alarm. She came home. She even made muffins! Hm! These are good."

Mother Anna took a muffin from the plate and sniffed it. "Was this—is this your mother's recipe?"

"Mm-hm!" Tanya nodded, even though she knew it wasn't exactly true, and that she'd had to guess some parts.

Mother Anna chewed and said, "Not bad."

"They're great," Pavel mumbled.

Other hands went to the plate.

"They're tasty, Tanya," said another of the women from the village.

They were all eating her muffins. Pavel had already finished his.

"What I need now is tea to wash that down," he

said. "Tanya, why don't you make some more of those muffins?"

And make more she did—five more batches that day. Other villagers came to the house. They came expecting to see a sad little girl, but instead they found a busy girl mixing batter and pouring it into muffin pans and making muffins. Everyone got one. It was like a party, and the only ones missing were Tanya's parents. People were milling about in the kitchen and out in the sunny barnyard, eating and talking and drinking tea. Tanya looked up from her latest batch of batter, and through the windowpanes she saw Pavel standing at the gate, holding half a muffin and waving to someone down the road.

"Hey!" Pavel whistled. "Come and taste something!"

For a moment Tanya thought he was calling to her mother and father.

CHAPTER

FIVE

But her parents didn't come that day, or the next day or the day after that. She stopped looking down the road. On the third day, she walked with Milenka to the high meadow at the top of the field. She looked out past the countryside toward the sea, a thin silver line under a cloudy sky.

It was a long way to the sea. Her father had told her that someone in the village once dropped a wooden box in the river and that a fisherman found it floating in the sea. That was what must have happened to her parents, and that was why they were taking so long. Tanya told herself a story about her parents. They had lost the horse and the wagon but not each other. The river had washed them into the sea, and a fisherman had picked them up in his boat. The fisherman had taken them ashore, but it was still a long way home.

On any other day she would be looking down from the high meadow and seeing the tiny figure of her mother going to the well, or her father chopping wood. There was something comforting about the sound of her father chopping wood—so steady, like a big clock ticking outdoors.

Now the big sound was the cawing of the crows, those crows her father always had to chase away. The crows ruled the field. They perched in the trees and yelled to each other, flew every which way and pecked at the corn and wheat. Tanya sat in the high meadow while Milenka grazed. The cowbell clanked each time Milenka took another step and nuzzled the grass.

"Milenka, come," Tanya said, and Milenka followed her down the hillside.

They went the orchard way. The wind beat her skirt against the backs of her legs and plucked a ripe apple from a tree. Tanya remembered the last time she had helped her father pick apples. It was last fall. Her father was up in a tree, tossing apples into the bushel basket Tanya was carrying. Gently, playfully, he threw an apple down so it bounced on Tanya's head, and she ran crying to the house. Her father found her on her bed, took her in his arms, and apologized. Now, walking with Milenka along the edge of the scraggly trees, Tanya wished she were crying again over that silly apple and being held by her father.

She thought of the last thing he said to her on the

bridge, how he scolded her about leaving the barn door open. He had sounded so angry. She wished he hadn't spoken to her like that. She hadn't done anything wrong. She'd forgotten about the barn door, that was all. He didn't have to shout at her.

The crows cawed, and the wind made Tanya untie the sweater from around her waist and put it on.

At least she didn't come home to an empty house. Mother Anna was staying with her, minding the house, and had brought her little Nikola. Nikola was Mother Anna's special child—Tanya could tell, by the way Mother Anna looked at him. Mother Anna had hard, little blue eyes that looked you up and down and didn't miss a thing. But her eyes would flutter back to Nikola like a bird to its nest, and the eyes would widen, and Tanya could see sadness and worry, and the gleam of tears.

The tears were there—Tanya could see them. Tanya had always known that Mother Anna fussed and fretted over Nikola, but she'd never noticed the tears in Mother Anna's eyes before. Something was happening to Tanya. She was seeing things she'd never seen, feeling things she'd never felt before.

Mother Anna slept in her parents' bed. Tanya didn't think her parents would mind because Mother Anna meant well, but it bothered her to hear the bed creak and then to have to remember who it was, and who it should have been. Mother Anna snored. The snoring would wake Tanya up, and Tanya would lie awake wondering if Mother Anna was in her father's or her mother's valley in the bed in the other room. But she never went to look. She only wanted to see her parents in that bed.

Nikola slept in there with Mother Anna, and sometimes Tanya would hear her speaking softly to him, calling him her baby boy and her boylet and her dearest baby heart, and telling him to go back to sleep. Tanya would turn on her side and imagine her parents sleeping in a barn somewhere, on a bed of hay, after another day of their hard journey home. And then the next thing she knew, it was light outside, and time to get out the muffin pans.

Making muffins always lifted Tanya's spirits. If she was feeling sad that day, or missing her parents more than she thought she could bear, she forgot her troubles when she made muffins. If there were crows outside, she stopped hearing them, and the only things on her mind were the soft flour, the eggs, the butter, the sugar, Milenka's milk, and the other things she put together in her own special way and handed over to the warm magic of the oven.

And then there were visitors, people coming by to say hello. They came all day. The shepherds came first, crowding the barnyard with their flocks and upsetting the geese. The shepherds would bring tangy cheese and olives and bread, and have breakfast at the house. The farmers stopped on the way to their fields to bring grapes and smoked ham. Pavel dropped by in the morning with fresh cheeses from Kosta the Cheesemaker, and Mother Anna's friends would come and make a big lunch with a leg of lamb or some grilled trout, beans and spinach, raisin bread, jam and honey.

There was so much food, so much eating; and still people asked for muffins.

"Any more of those muffins, Tanya?"

"So that's what I smell in the oven! Oh, I'll wait. I'm in no rush."

"Tanya, would you mind making us some of your muffins?"

"It keeps her busy," Mother Anna said to her friends; and while she breezed around the house and talked and made the big meals, Tanya made the muffins. Tanya liked making them, liked putting the hot muffins on a plate, then holding the plate in her hands and watching the muffins disappear before her eyes. She searched the cupboards for more muffin pans. Every fresh batch was gone in no time, and often she would be mixing more eggs and milk and butter in the bowl while there were still muffins in the oven, and the smell rose like the sun in the morning.

She went to the high meadow again late one day with Milenka, to gather wild blueberries. The blueberry bushes grew behind the meadow, along the edge of the black pines.

It was one of those days that promises no sun, and then just before sundown the sun finds a crack in the clouds and glances over the countryside. The orange light caught the insects floating over the grass. Tanya gazed seaward, then took the lane down the middle of the field. The corn was on one side, the wheat on the other.

The crows were excited, and Tanya saw two men walking up through the wheat. They were Pavel and another villager, a man called Stepan.

They stopped to pull wheat stalks, and then they rubbed their hands together and tasted it. Tanya knew what they were doing. They were sampling the wheat to see how close it was to harvesting. A good farmer could tell by the way the seeds broke open, and by the taste. Tanya had watched her father do it. But she didn't like Pavel and Stepan doing it, and she didn't think her father would like it either. She knew how he was about his field. She felt angry for him, angry in his place.

Pavel and Stepan crossed into the corn but didn't see her—she was higher up the lane, with Milenka in front of her. Tanya heard Pavel's voice.

"It's just too big a responsibility," Pavel was saying.

"How old is she? Ten? Eleven?" Stepan said.

They were talking about her. She held still and listened.

"Eleven," Pavel said.

Tanya wanted to shout: "Eleven going on twelve!" But she kept quiet, kept listening.

"Eleven *now,*" Pavel went on. "In a couple of years she'll be a handful. She's already a handful. She's at our house one night and she runs away! My wife doesn't mind staying out here for a little bit, but how long can this go on? She's got to have Nikola with her. She hates to let him out of her sight. Fine, but what about our other kids? We can't run two households."

"Mm."

"Mm! What's that supposed to mean? We need help here, Stepan. Everybody's saying, 'Oh, Mother Anna and Pavel have solved the Tanya problem. Wasn't that nice of them?' No. That's not the way it works. It can't all be on us. Other people have to share the burden. Either that, or we take the farm. If we're going to have another kid on our hands and a whole other mouth to feed, we deserve something for our trouble."

"Hold your horses," Stepan said. "That's a pretty high price for taking care of one little kid."

"The one paying the price will be me," Pavel said. "With two farms I'll have more work than I can handle. I'll have to hire people."

"Who says you have to hire people? We can divide up the place. Everybody gets a piece, and we take turns with the little girl."

"Right now, I'm the one who's stuck with her," Pavel

said. "We don't make any deals until this situation changes."

"This is a sweet farm," Stepan said. "Don't think you're going to have it all to yourself."

In the lane, Milenka flicked her tail and pulled another tuft of grass. Tanya heard the men snap an ear of corn from a stalk and rip the husk off. Now they were quiet. They were looking at the corn. If you pinched it with your thumbnail and a little squirt of juice came out, that meant the corn was ripe.

"Three more days of sun, and this corn's ready," Stepan said. "It's going to be a nice crop."

"Very nice," Pavel said. "Those two picked the wrong time to go for a swim."

CHAPTER
SIX

It was harvest time: that time of year when the wheat was cut and tied up in shocks to dry. The shocks standing in rows looked like people, like soldiers standing guard. But there were no soldiers to guard the farm this year, and Tanya had to fight her battles by herself.

Early the next day—the morning after Tanya over-heard Pavel and Stepan in the field—Pavel came to the house. Stepan and his wife came, and Kosta the Cheesemaker and his wife came, all at once. They brought a lunch of roast turkey and stuffed peppers, and helped themselves to hot muffins. The grownups talked village talk—who hadn't been feeling well lately, who was going to have a baby, whose daughter was about to marry whose son. Tanya hardly listened. She was thinking about what she'd heard Pavel and Stepan saying about the harvest coming, and she felt very alone.

Nikola sat on the floor playing with his blocks, click clack, click clack. Tanya watched him.

Mother Anna said, "We have a special present for you, dear."

At first, Tanya thought Mother Anna was talking to Nikola. She looked up and saw Mother Anna holding a little box, like a jewelry box.

"Did you hear what I said, dear? We have a present for you."

Tanya held her breath as she took the box in both hands and lifted the lid.

The box was empty.

"Isn't it beautiful?" said Mother Helena, who was Stepan's wife.

"Look at how beautiful it is," Mother Anna said, pointing at the roses and stars all over the box. Mother Anna had thick red fingers like sausages, with tight little gold rings on them.

"The roses and stars are made of tiny pieces of precious things. The roses are made of tiny pieces of sandalwood and cedar, and the stars are mother-of-pearl. Do you know what mother-of-pearl is?"

"Mm-hm," Tanya said, not because she knew, but because she was so disappointed and didn't know what to say.

"Mother-of-pearl comes from the inside of the shell of an oyster."

"From the bottom of the sea," said Pavel.

The mother-of-pearl was shiny, like the silver gleam of the sea when Tanya looked from the high meadow.

"This was brought to our country by ship," Stepan said.

"It's very rare," Mother Anna said. "Something to treasure all your life."

"Oh, I will treasure it," Tanya said.

"Tanya," Pavel said, "we'd like to talk to you about something."

"Yes?"

They were all staring at her. Nikola's blocks went click clack, and a crow in the trees nearby was calling to its friends.

"It's about the farm," Pavel said.

Tanya sat and listened as they talked to her about the farm. She held the box in her hands and listened to them say things she already knew. About how hard her father had worked, how tired he would be at the end of each day, and how proud he was of his harvest every year.

She didn't need them to tell her that. They never climbed onto his lap and smelled the earth and his sweat. They never poured the hot water for his foot-bath. They never danced with him around the kitchen with a stalk of baby wheat behind their ears. She answered them silently, in her heart.

"But it all comes from God, Tanya," Pavel said. "Your father knew that. No matter how hard we work, the harvest is God's blessing. And it's wrong to let the harvest go to waste."

There was no time to lose, they said. In a few days the corn and wheat and apples would start to rot. The crows were already on the attack.

Everything they said was right, but somehow it all sounded wrong. Tanya wished she could have asked her father what to do. She closed her eyes and tried to see him, tried to listen for his voice. Nothing happened. She opened her eyes, and the villagers were still staring at her.

"Are you listening, dear?" Mother Anna said.

Tanya said: "What will my father say when he comes back?"

A look of pity passed over Mother Anna's face. "But, dear . . . "

Pavel spoke next. "Tanya, don't you think this is what your father would have wanted?"

"I only want to see my father in the field," Tanya said, and cast her eyes down at the box in her hands. She could feel the adults glancing at each other. Nikola banged his blocks, and Mother Anna picked him up and put him on her lap. She moved so quickly, Nikola dropped one of his blocks, and he began to cry and screech.

"Oh Nikola, my dearest, dearest," Mother Anna moaned. Pavel frowned and rushed to pick up the block. But he didn't seem to know what to do with it. He gave it to Mother Anna to give to Nikola. Mother Anna went on: "Momma has your block! Momma has it! Here, see? Here it is for you! Everything's fine now, my dearest darling boy, my beautiful little boylo."

Mother Anna with Nikola was like Nikola with his blocks: when she had him in her arms, there was nothing else in the world. The other grownups looked on, all except Pavel. He turned and stared out the window.

The adults stepped outside. Mother Anna took Nikola with her. Through the windowpanes Tanya could see them by the barn, see Nikola being held, with his arms around his mother, his red face on her shoulder and his blocks in his fists as she patted his back.

They tried to talk in hushed voices, but their voices would rise, and they talked the way grownups talk, as though the children around them don't have ears. Tanya couldn't hear everything they said, just something about "taking turns staying out here," and something about the wheat and how little time there was, and Mother Anna saying: "Such a stubborn child!"

Tanya felt awkward and confused. Perhaps they were really trying to do what was best. She didn't want the harvest to go to waste, and she knew her father wouldn't have wanted that either. She still held the little box Mother Anna had given her. It truly was a beautiful box. Had she been ungrateful?

As the others left, Mother Anna came back into the house with Nikola. Tanya thanked her for the box.

"You're quite welcome," Mother Anna replied stiffly.

The others' footsteps went out the gate, and then a single pair came trotting back. Pavel appeared at the door.

"Wasn't there a muffin left over? Tanya, could I have it?"

"Oh, please, take it!" Tanya gave it to him. "Would you like me to make more?"

"Pavel!" Mother Anna said. "Go on home!"

CHAPTER
SEVEN

They came two days later to cut the wheat. Twenty men from the village came with scythes and started cutting at the top of the field, working their way downhill. No one asked Tanya or even warned her. That morning, she had gone back to sleep after milking Milenka, and she awoke a little before noon. She found Mother Anna in the kitchen downstairs, but Mother Anna didn't speak to her. Tanya went outside, beyond the barn, and saw the line of men up along the curve of the hill, the men swinging their arms, swaying behind the wheat.

It was a warm day, and the grasshoppers were hopping in front of her like popcorn popping as she ran. Halfway up the hill, she could smell the nutty smell of the fresh-cut wheat. The men gripped the long handles of the scythes, and the wheat fell to the swishing of the blades.

"What are you doing?" Tanya shouted.

"What's it look like?" one of the men said.

Another stopped and passed a handkerchief over his sweaty face. "You didn't bring us any water, did you? I thought you brought us water."

"Tanya." Pavel left the line to come over to her. He hoisted his scythe over his shoulder, the blade up in the air. Behind him—behind them all—spread a carpet of fallen wheat, the smell so wild and delicious, it almost made you dizzy.

"I was going to tell you," Pavel said, "but you were asleep."

"My father will kill you when he finds out."

"What are you talking about?" Pavel said. "We do this sometimes. We go to each other's farms and help out with the harvest."

"And you're going to take it all away, aren't you?" Tanya said.

"We'll give you a share of what we make out of this, don't you worry."

Tanya turned away. Her eyes burned with tears, and in her thoughts she said to Pavel and the others: "Just you wait. Just you wait."

Pavel called after her: "Did you make any muffins today, Tanya? Why don't you make us some muffins?"

The others picked up the cry.

"Yeah, make us some muffins, Tanya!"

"Oh, come on! Don't be like that!"

"We really like them a lot."

"We're working up a big appetite. When's lunch, anyway?"

She did make muffins for them, because she felt helpless. She was little, they were big; she was one, they were many. They were everywhere. Mother Anna was in the house, where her mother should have been. Nikola banged his blocks. After their lunch the men sprawled on the grass like they owned the place. They strode around with their scythes up on their shoulders, and talked about the barn and the field and the orchard and the duck pond and the woods and what they were going to do with it all. Tanya made four batches of muffins and went up to her room and shut the door. As she lay on her bed, she told herself this wouldn't last forever, her parents would soon set things straight, they would never be friends with the villagers again, and the villagers would be sorry.

When she awoke from another dreamless sleep— she'd slept half the day away—it was past sunset. She went downstairs to find Nikola with his blocks and Mother Anna by the hearth, knitting. Mother Anna was in a bad mood. She didn't lift her eyes as Tanya came down the steps, and there was something sour about her way with the knitting needles, the way they clicked in her impatient hands.

There was a stewpot on the hearth. Tanya lifted the lid.

"Well!" Mother Anna said. "You're up, finally."

Tanya sniffed inside the pot. She didn't like the smell of it. She didn't like Mother Anna's cooking.

"You're welcome to what's left, dear. We left it for you."

"No, thank you," Tanya said, and went toward the door.

"Now where are you going?"

"I'm going outside for a while."

"You can wait a moment, can't you? I have to talk to you."

Mother Anna kept knitting as she talked. "I didn't want to waken you or leave while you were asleep. I'm needed at home, dear. I need to be back home to mind my other children and take care of my own house. Nikola and I will be leaving in a few minutes. You're welcome to come with us if you don't want to be alone tonight."

"I'll be fine," Tanya said.

"I thought so. The men will be back in the morning, and Mother Helena will be staying with you tomorrow night. She'll be here for a few days. Then it will be someone else's turn. We'll all take turns."

"All right."

"We'll take turns for a while, and then we'll have to make some more permanent arrangement. You can't live out here all by yourself. You may have to come live with us or with some other family in the village. Or we may move out here. It's a big farm, and it just doesn't make any sense any other way."

Tanya didn't understand what a "permanent arrangement" was—what that meant, exactly—but she knew it didn't have her parents in it. Never mind. Mother Anna would go away soon. The villagers would all go away soon. They were like a bad smell that would go away when her parents came back and opened the windows.

"Don't you have anything to say?" Mother Anna said.

"Thank you, Mother Anna."

"Come over here before I go and give me a kiss."

Nikola didn't look up from his blocks when Tanya said goodbye to him. She went out under the twilight, glad to be outside, gladder still that she was getting her house back, at least for one night. Having other people around didn't help anymore. Somehow she felt closer to her mother and father when there was no one in sight, no one to get in the way of her thoughts about them.

Maybe, she thought, they would be home tonight, waiting for her when she came back to the house.

She let Milenka out of the barn, and together the little girl and the spotted cow went up the lane between the corn and wheat, to see what the men had done.

The wheat was half cut, the smell of it still strong. The men had gathered and tied what they had cut, and the shocks climbed in rows to the high meadow. Over the mountains hung a fat harvest moon. Something sailed under the moon, something white and silent, like the owl that lived in the barn.

"I think that's your neighbor, Milenka."

There were no crows after dark, but the crickets were going wild. They all seemed to be peeping and squeaking behind the wall of corn. A day or two more, and the men would harvest the corn. They would come back in the morning, take another day cutting the wheat, and then start on the corn. Tanya slipped into the cornfield.

The leaves and the cornsilk felt like paper and rags brushing against her, and the smell of corn surrounded her. The moon watched her.

She broke an ear from a stalk, peeled the husk part way, and pinched the kernels. She could feel the juice on her thumb. She walked along, taking some more corn for herself, and she thought how angry her father was going to be when he found out about the men taking his crop. She knew his anger. She'd felt it herself, felt it flowing through her.

But she was worried about him being angry at her too. He was already angry at her for leaving the barn door open that night on the bridge—and now this. It was his farm but it was her job to watch over it, and she was letting them steal his harvest. She thought of what she would say to him when his eyes passed over the field and hardened with anger and turned in her direction. She'd tell him she couldn't stop them. She hoped he would understand. But what about the muffins she'd made? She'd treated the villagers like guests, not like the thieves they really were. How would she explain that?

Why did she hear her father's voice when she least expected it? Even the crickets fell silent and listened—or at least Tanya didn't hear them anymore as her thoughts went back to a time in her life when the corn was taller than now. She was with her father that late-summer day a long time ago, hopping down the lane between the corn and wheat, making the grasshoppers hop in front of her.

Her father was carrying a bushel of corn, and she had asked him why he didn't just give the corn to people.

"If I did that, sweetness, we'd be poor," he explained, with a bit of a groan to his voice because the bushel basket was heavy. "Instead, I make people pay me for what I give them. They give me money, and that way, we have money to buy things."

"Oh, I see."

"My Tanya, never let people take advantage of you," he went on, and though she didn't understand him then, she did now. "If you have something people want and it's good, make them appreciate you and pay a fair price."

"Milenka!" Tanya said, dashing from the corn. Milenka's white spots glowed red in the moonlight. The cow lifted her head with a clank of her bell and looked at Tanya.

"I know what we'll do!"

CHAPTER
EIGHT

The first to pay for a muffin was Anton the Sharpener. Anton made the rounds of the village and the farms, sharpening blades. Everyone knew the gawky, stooped figure of Anton with the grindstone on his back. He carried it wherever he went. It had shoulder straps, a wooden stand, and a pedal. He would find something to sit on, set his grindstone on the ground, step on the pedal and do his work, then hoist it on his back again and walk on with his walking stick, as though on a Sunday stroll.

Tanya never knew a time when there wasn't Anton, and she grew up thinking he could have left his grindstone home and used his nose instead, because it was big and sharp and looked hard as rock. But Anton without his grindstone wouldn't have been Anton. Wherever Anton was, there was the squeal of metal on stone, and his voice, like a song, soft and beautiful to listen to, an unlikely voice from such an ungainly man.

"Good morning, good morning," Anton said, leaning down through the kitchen's roadside window. "A sharp blade, and your fortune is made. Wouldn't life be dull without Anton?"

Tanya knew all of Anton's silly rhymes and tired old jokes. Sometimes she couldn't tell whether he was picking on her or trying to be friendly.

"Just came up from down the road, and did a lady spider a favor this morning. Such a pretty web she had, draped between two fenceposts and all covered with dew. But she needed another. So Anton sharpened a blade of grass and sliced that web lengthwise. Now she has two. Gave her half-price on the dewdrops. Pretty keen, wouldn't you say?"

"I just made some muffins, Anton. Would you like one?"

"I've heard about these muffins, child. I've heard."

"Here you are," Tanya said; then, resting her elbows on the windowsill, she cupped her chin in her hands and listened to him talk.

Because he went from house to house, Anton knew everyone's business, and had all the latest gossip.

"Let's see, what's new?" he began, picking off pieces of muffin with his fingers. "Slava's mare had her foal last night."

"I want to see it! Is it a boy or a girl?"

"A girl. They named her Daisy-in-the-Meadow. And what else? Oh! Vlado found out what was wrong with his field."

"There was something wrong with it?"

"There certainly was. Didn't you hear? His beans were dying on him. He thought he'd lost his whole field. The trouble started two weeks ago. First the beans stopped growing, then they wilted and withered for no reason, and it was quite a mystery to him. He showed the other farmers and they all talked about it. They said it was Gypsies."

"Gypsies!" Tanya said.

"Yes, Gypsies, up to no good. They're very clever poisoners, you know. Except we haven't had Gypsies lately. We've been lucky. Well, Gypsies or no Gypsies, Vlado feared the worst. Until yesterday, that is. He was walking in his field with his dog, and the dog started digging. Vlado called the dog. The dog barked at him and kept digging with its paws. What do you think they found? A clay pot wrapped in cloth, with twine around it. And inside the pot was a dead toad stuffed with barley."

Tanya straightened up in alarm.

"Quite so. Vlado burned the toad to ashes, hammered the pot to pieces, put it all in a sack, and threw the sack into a cave. And this morning his beans have already bounced back."

"How did the toad get there?"

"Someone put it there. Someone went to a witch, and the witch put the hex together and told him to plant it in Vlado's field."

"Who's the witch?"

"That's an interesting question. I don't know. Witches don't go around advertising. They're quite secretive, actually. If you go to a witch, a real witch, she'll send you away, and make you come back a couple of times before she'll even listen to you. And then, before she does anything, she makes you pay, first in gold and then with a lock of your own hair, so that if you ever tell anyone about her, she'll put a hex on *you*. Someday"—Anton licked his fingers—"someday, child, you will make your husband very happy."

"Did you enjoy the muffin, Anton?"

"Extremely."

"Then I want you to pay me something."

For once, Anton seemed at a loss for words. Tanya said:

"You make people pay you when you sharpen things for them. Why shouldn't you pay me for the muffin?"

"Haven't you heard of hospitality?"

"If I keep giving muffins away, I'll have nothing."

"Infallible logic of the child," Anton muttered to himself. Then: "So be it. Price of muffin?"

"Five pence will be fine."

Anton dug deep into his pocket, counted out the coins, and paid for his muffin. But he made more than he paid that morning. When the men came for the wheat-cutting, he sharpened all their blades. He could have done it in the sunlight, but there you couldn't see the sparks; he sat on the milking stool inside the barn. Anton liked working in the shadows, where the green sparks winked and spat as the metal met his grindstone and grated on your nerves. Tanya liked to watch, but up close the noise bothered her, so she climbed the ladder to the hayloft and sat there, looking down, her feet dangling and her fingers over her ears. The men formed a loose line to Anton. Each man bent down to hold his scythe in place, while Anton's fingers wiped the blade over his spinning, rumbling stone wheel.

As Anton worked, he talked to each customer but spoke down to the blade, like a dentist talking to your teeth. He was chatty, full of news, and had something to say to everyone; and it was Anton who announced that Tanya was now charging for her muffins.

"What!" the first man in the line said.

"Oh, didn't you know?" Anton said over his sparks. "The price has gone up. Was nothing. Now it's five pence."

The blade lifted from the grindstone, and the news rippled down the line.

"You hear that? Tanya wants money for the muffins."

"You're kidding."

"How much?"

"Five pence."

"The muffins aren't free anymore."

"She wants money."

"Who gave her that idea?"

"How much?"

"Ten pence."

"Where is she? Where'd she go?"

"*Twenty* pence? For one muffin?"

"There she is! Up there!"

The barn echoed like a cave, and the men's voices had grown quite loud.

"Tanya! What's this about charging for muffins? Is it true?"

"Yes!" Tanya said, looking down at their upturned faces.

"Well, how much?"

"Five pence."

"They said it was twenty."

"Just five." She showed five fingers.

Pavel was standing out in the barnyard, but the commotion brought him inside. He listened for a moment, then:

"Tanya, are you sure you want to do this?"

"Yes!" Tanya came down the ladder and faced all the men with their scythes. Pavel looked at her with a hard glint in his eye and stroked his moustache.

Anton spoke up. "A bit of business sense never did hurt a child."

"Anton," Pavel said, "how much are you robbing us these days?"

"It depends. Five pence for each scissor blade, ten for every knife. Twenty for a sickle, twenty-five for a scythe. Cutlasses and sabers to be negotiated."

"Five pence for a muffin won't break me," Pavel said. "Come on, guys, let's pay for our muffins. Let Tanya have some fun."

"Sure, why not? The poor kid."

"Do we get a baker's dozen?" said another man.

"What's that?" Tanya said.

"It's thirteen for the price of twelve. They throw one in for free."

"All right."

By the end of the day, thirty-six muffins had changed hands. Actually, the number was thirty-nine, counting the three extras for the baker's dozens. When the money from the first dozen came in, Tanya squeezed the coins in her fist and jumped up and down with happiness. With the third dozen she had more money than she knew what to do with. Where should she put it all? On the kitchen table was the box Mother Anna had given her. Tanya dropped the coins inside and paused to think about where the box should go. After a moment's thought, she knew.

She went up the stairs and turned the doorknob to her parents' room. Their wardrobe stood to the right as she entered. It was painted blue and gold, and smelled of quince and lavender inside. Tanya hid the box under a pile of linen sheets and pillowcases, next to a little pouch of lavender. Closing the panels, she turned to look at her parents' bed, the bed that remembered their shapes so well. She sent a thought its way: "I can't wait to tell you."

Sometime that day, someone called her the Muffin Child—though the name didn't take hold until later, when the countryside turned the color of rust, the wind grew scratchy with leaves, and her parents still hadn't come home. People from farms and villages over the hills knew who the Muffin Child was. She was that little girl on the abandoned farm, the orphan who believed her parents were still alive, struggling homeward on muddy roads in harsh weather. She was not like other children, but solitary, gifted, and dangerous.

CHAPTER
NINE

Dangerous, they said; and it started when she made a mess of the harvest.

It took the men a couple of days to finish cutting and tying the wheat. On the afternoon of the second day, as the work was winding down, they went to the well for a drink and a splash on their faces, and trudged around the barn to head homeward, carrying their scythes on their shoulders. Tanya was feeding the geese. Pavel and Stepan were among the last to go, and when she saw them going, she said:

"Pavel, when are you going to pay me for my father's wheat?"

"*Pay* you?" Pavel said. "I've been paying you all day."

"That's for muffins. What about my father's wheat?"

"What about it?"

"It's his field, and his wheat," Tanya said.

"And my aching back."

"You said you'd give me something for the harvest. You said so yesterday."

"You think we're running a charity here?" Pavel said.

"It's not for me, it's for my father."

Pavel walked on, without so much as a glance at her. She said to his back:

"What are you going to say to him when he sees you?"

No answer.

"I can't believe this kid," Stepan said.

Stepan's wife, Mother Helena, was supposed to come that evening and stay with Tanya, but she never showed up. Once again, Tanya had the place to herself. She went out to look at the field again.

There was a sprinkle of rain. The day's warmth still hung on the wind; it was getting dark, and the clouds had a stormy green glow. Pink flashes of lightning pulsed behind the clouds.

Tanya looked up at the field full of wheat shocks in their neat rows. She wished she could make them come to life, make them march away and hide deep in the woods until her father came back.

In her mind she saw it happen. With a tramping of their wheaty legs, the shocks filed up the hillside into the black pines. Row by row they went—and then, as though she were turning the pages of a picture book, turning back to the picture on the first page, the shocks were all back again. They hadn't budged. The wind toyed with their loose ends.

Tanya couldn't make the shocks go away, but she did what she could. She went to the barn and got her father's pruning shears and a rake, and she brought Milenka out to watch. Milenka stood in the lane with the cornstalks behind her. With her father's shears, Tanya cut the strings that tied the shocks. She used the rake to tip them over, and she pushed the wheat this way and that, spreading it around again. The clouds flickered with silent lights.

This was hard work, and Tanya only got to about half of the shocks. Some she just knocked over and kicked a little. She tired herself out, and the rake hurt her hands. She knew she'd have blisters in the morning, and she knew the villagers wouldn't like what she'd done. But she'd done what she could to keep her father's wheat on the farm.

"When will the muffins be ready?" Pavel said in the morning as he entered the house without knocking. Tanya was stirring batter, trying not to pop the blisters on her hands as she gripped the big wooden spoon.

"Soon," she said, and her face felt hot and her heart knocked against her ribs, because in a few minutes they would all find out what she'd done.

"Where's Mother Helena?" Pavel said.

"She didn't come."

"What?" A look of irritation crossed Pavel's face. Without another word he went outside and paced in the barnyard, trailing smoke from his pipe. Tanya looked at him through the windowpanes. All he had to do was go around the other side of the barn. But he didn't just yet.

Stepan and some of the others came next, each with a stack of empty bushel baskets under his arm. There were fewer men today. They were planning on picking corn.

"Stepan!" Pavel said, clenching his pipe between his teeth. "What happened to Helena?"

"I meant to tell you," Stepan said. "Something came up. She couldn't make it." And the two of them started arguing over who should have been there last night to take care of Tanya and who was going to be there tonight and tomorrow night and the week after. Tanya put a muffin pan in the oven and listened to them. They wanted the harvest. They wanted the farm. They just didn't want her.

"We had a deal," she heard Pavel tell Stepan. "We share the harvest, we share the little girl. If that's not going to be the way it works—"

The other men didn't want to get involved. They had their own fields, their own families to take care of. They drifted away, leaving Pavel and Stepan to argue in the barnyard.

But the two didn't have to argue much longer. As soon as the others walked around the barn, they saw the wheat field, and they came back with the news. And from that moment onward, no one worried anymore about who was going to take care of Tanya.

"You little witch," Pavel said.

She was a brat, a spiteful girl, the kind of girl who would rather see the wheat rot and feed the crows than go to the people who'd tried to help her. That was how they saw it. So they took what they wanted. They took the shocks of wheat still standing and piled them onto carts. They went through the cornfield and picked corn, each man filling his own baskets. They brought the ladder to the orchard and pulled the ripe apples from the branches. It was a sloppy harvest. No one cut down the cornstalks, and they left Tanya's scattered wheat on the ground.

All to teach her a lesson, to show her what happened when you didn't respect anything or anybody. And when she got desperate, then they would have their way, they'd have the farm. Time was on their side. Winter was on its way, and they knew she'd come running to them when the cold set in.

"I'll give her till the first hard frost," one said.

"It can get pretty lonely in a house all by yourself in the winter," said another.

Those farmers knew how to save their dander and

their sweat. It was like everything else they did. Why push a plow when you could hitch it to a horse? Take it easy. Give it time. And what were they dealing with, anyway? Just a kid.

CHAPTER
TEN

But the villagers hadn't lost their taste for Tanya's muffins. Three days after Pavel called her a little witch and drove off with a cartload of wheat, the latch turned in the door, and it was Pavel again.

On the table he dropped a wicker basket. Loaves and potatoes and cheese and eggplants were sticking out of the top of it.

"I don't want you to starve."

Tanya was wary, a little afraid. She thought Pavel was angry at her.

He opened her mother's cupboards. "There's plenty of food here. Your momma ran a good house. You got everything you need for muffins?"

"I think so."

He sniffed and held his hand over the oven. "You're

making some right now, aren't you? You put them in a minute ago."

"Yes."

"I'll pay you, all right? Just to prove I'm not a bad guy, I'll pay you for muffins."

As he waited, Tanya went out to the woodpile in the barnyard and brought firewood into the kitchen, stacking the pieces in the alcove beside the hearth.

"I come over here and bring you free food, and I don't even ask for free muffins," Pavel said. "Think about that. Let it sink in."

She served him muffins.

"Gosh, these are good," Pavel said. "Whip me up another batch and I'll take them with me. What, you don't believe me? Here."

He pulled a fistful of coins from his pocket. "Another batch makes a dozen muffins total. Five pence each. Twelve times five is sixty." On the table he counted out the coins. "Ten, twenty, twenty-five, thirty, thirty-five, forty, forty-five . . . sixty. I won't even ask for a baker's dozen."

She stirred the batter and listened to him talk.

"Imagine you had a donkey, Tanya. You ride the donkey everywhere and you're happy with it because you don't know any better. Somebody comes along and gives you a racehorse—for a week. Then they take the racehorse away. Who wants to get back on the donkey?"

Pavel saw that she didn't understand, and he went on: "Mother Anna's feeding me and the kids the same muffins she's been making for years. Don't get me wrong, Mother Anna's a good woman. I used to think her muffins were fine. But yours are just better, that's all. I don't know what it is."

Pavel's basket left the house lighter. He unloaded all the food he'd brought, and he put nine muffins (three left over from the first batch, plus the other six) into the basket. The muffins were wrapped in grape leaves to keep them fresh.

"Why do you want all those muffins, Pavel?" Tanya asked.

"Some of the other guys were talking about it and said they wanted a taste. If you see Mother Anna, don't say anything about this. You promise me?"

"I promise."

"Not a word. You can say I was here, but keep the muffins out of it."

Instead of going out the gate, Pavel left the back way. Fallen yellow leaves crunched under his feet as he stepped toward the trees behind the house. He threw one leg after the other over the little wall of stacked fieldstones and vanished inside the birches, while angry crows flapped away and cawed.

CHAPTER
ELEVEN

Tanya couldn't figure it out. First Pavel called her names, now he was her friend. First he wouldn't pay a single pence for her father's wheat, now he paid for muffins, and slinked off into the birches like a little boy with a sack of stolen eggs. Tanya didn't understand him, but then she didn't understand anything anymore. It was better not to try to understand. Better to go about her chores and eat and sleep and get up the next day and do the same things all over again, and wait for her parents to put the world back in order.

She milked Milenka, fed the geese and chickens, gathered the day's eggs. She cleaned the coops and changed the hay. She swept the house. She did her chores because she knew her parents expected it while they were away. She still felt bad about the night on the bridge, when her father had yelled at her for not bolting the barn door. Tanya wanted to do everything just right from now on.

She was always so sleepy after her day that she fell asleep as soon as she got in bed. She went to bed at sunset.

Meanwhile, every day, men from the village came for muffins. Some gobbled them up as though they hadn't had food for days. Others sniffed the muffins like a glass of wine, then bit off little pieces and munched reflectively. They all came and went the back way, through the woods, and they told her not to tell their wives.

"Can you keep a secret?"

"Don't let Mother Helena know about this. I don't want to hurt her feelings."

"This is between you and me and that woodpile over there."

"Mum, not muffins. No muffins involved. Mum. You follow?"

"Remember what I said about Mother Anna."

"Mother Nina's tummy's been upset lately. She's nervous. Cranky. If you happen to see her, just say hello and leave it at that. Don't make conversation."

"This is for the muffins"—slapping a stack of coins in her hand—"and for you to keep your mouth shut!"

Another regular was Anton the Sharpener. Anton would stop by in the morning on his way up the road.

He'd finish off a muffin, crack one of his weak jokes—"Well, I suppose I'd better *look sharp,* as they say"—and come for a second taste on his way back. Except that Anton never asked Tanya to swear to secrecy. Anton was a bachelor and didn't have to worry.

Little Nikola came one afternoon, but he didn't want muffins. He was just wandering. Nikola did that sometimes. He'd be playing with his blocks under his mother's eyes, and suddenly he'd be off somewhere, going nowhere but astray. Everyone in the village and nearby farms knew to keep a lookout for Nikola and point him homeward, because Mother Anna became frantic if he was gone for long.

Tanya took him by the hand.

"Nikola, where are you going?"

She brought him inside and sat him by the table. He pulled his two blocks from his pocket. Click clack.

"Here, Nikola." She held a muffin under Nikola's nose. He didn't look up. She lifted his chin.

"Just taste it."

He bit into it, taking Tanya's finger in his teeth.

"Ow, Nikola!" Tanya put the muffin on the table. "Eat it by yourself."

Instead, he put one of his blocks on it, and balanced the other block on top of the first.

"Don't play with it."

He slammed the blocks on the muffin.

"Nikola, stop!"

She snatched his blocks away. That was a mistake. His cheeks turned red and he whined, wheezed, pounded the table with the flat of his hands, pounding the muffin to pieces.

It frightened her to watch him. She gave him back his blocks, and he sobbed to himself as he went on playing, his long black lashes soaked with tears. Tanya gazed at Nikola, and tried to see Nikola's world. She thought of Maya, her doll. When Tanya was five, she would feed Maya three times a day with a spoon and a cup. There was nothing on the spoon or in the cup, but that didn't matter, Maya understood. Maya was still upstairs in Tanya's room, sitting in a tiny chair her father had made. But Tanya was more grown up now, and Maya got along by herself. Maybe Nikola's blocks were like Maya, Tanya thought. Maybe they were dolls to him, and needed taking care of.

Nikola shivered and sighed over his blocks. The firelight twinkled on his wet cheek.

"Nikola, it's time to go now. It'll be dark soon, and you need to go home. Put your blocks away." She grabbed the blocks from Nikola's hands, and his little world started to come apart in the moment it took her to shove the blocks into his pocket. Then he was all right, and Tanya led him out to the road.

"Go home, Nikola."

She held him by the shoulders and gave him a little push.

Nikola went home. He went down the road, down the hill under the rays of the setting sun. They fanned out from behind the clouds. Smoke was rising from the village chimneys. Nikola hung his head. He didn't see the sunset or the twenty strings of smoke rising straight from those rooftops across the river, like strings on marionettes. Perhaps with a tug from God above, the village would dance on those strings of smoke. Nikola didn't see the beauty around him, but Tanya couldn't help wishing she could climb inside his heart and soul, just for a day.

"Your mommy's waiting for you," she called out after him; and she went inside to make the day's last batch of muffins. The last batch was always for her parents, in case they came home that night.

CHAPTER
TWELVE

Where *are* they?" she asked Milenka.

Another morning, and Tanya was in the barn, milking Milenka. The squirts pinged inside the metal pail. The pail was cold, and Tanya heard the calling of wild geese as they flew over the barn, on their way south. She laid her head against Milenka's ribs.

"What's taking them so long?"

Tanya went back to her milking, and the barn owl returned from the night, landing with a soft bump in the hayloft.

That was what didn't make any sense. How the rest of the world could go on as before. How the sun could keep rising and setting and Milenka giving milk. How the night could spit out an owl in the morning, like those furry pellets the owls left in the hayloft; and still no sign of her mother and father.

Last night's stale muffins were on the kitchen table. She fed them to the geese. The geese waddled toward her in a tight little knot as though they were all stuck together. They had only to see her with the plate in her hand, and they came squawking. The geese knew she had something for them, but they didn't know what it meant to her, and she hated them as she looked down at them gobbling the pieces of muffins from the dirt of the barnyard. They were getting so fat.

She went into the house and stood by the hearth, to feel the warmth and to wonder about her parents. It always helped to look into a fire. It made you think there was more than just what you could see. Tanya still believed that when her parents were washed into the sea, a fisherman had found them. But maybe when the fisherman had taken them to the shore of his land, it was another land, on another side of the water. Maybe her parents had caught colds in the water, and they had to wait until they were both feeling well enough to travel. They were stranded there, they had no money, and no one spoke their language. They had to wait, and so did she. They wouldn't come today or tomorrow. It might be weeks before they came. It might be winter. It might even be spring.

Still, she went ahead and made muffins. She took Milenka's milk and the morning's butter and eggs, and she started. The first batch of the day, like the last, was always for her parents. She knew she had to do that. She knew she had to think that way. If she stopped making muffins for her parents, then sooner or later they would find out, and when the sun rose at last on the day of their return, they would be so hurt, because it meant that she'd given up on them. She could never do that.

The quilt on their bed had a rip in it. Tanya didn't know whether Mother Anna and Nikola had made it when they slept on the bed, or whether the culprit was simply time. Anyway, she folded up the quilt and took it downstairs and sat by the hearth with needle and thread and the hissing fire to keep her company.

"Psst."

Tanya didn't move, because it sounded like the hiss of the fire.

"Tanya."

Pavel was at the back window. There were tall, burry weeds under that window, and he was pulling burrs off his pants.

"Pavel, what are you doing? Are you hiding?"

He saw the batch of muffins on the table and said: "I'll have one now and take the rest with me."

She brought the plate to the window. Pavel dumped all but one of the muffins into his haversack.

"Apple cinnamon. My favorite." Munching, he said: "You trust me, right? I mean, have I ever been stingy about paying you? Have I ever cheated you? Just the opposite. I've been throwing money at you. So don't get the wrong idea about what I'm going to say. Now, Tanya. Did your parents keep any money buried anywhere?"

"I don't think so."

"Listen to me. Everybody hides money. Everybody has a secret hiding place. Maybe it's under a floor, or inside a mattress, or—or under a stone somewhere, or in some little hole under a root in the orchard. Listen, if you tore up every floor in our village, ripped open every mattress, and dug up every orchard, you'd find a fortune in gold."

He slapped the muffin crumbs off his hands. Then he waved his hands as if to say stop.

"I know, I'm going too fast. I just don't want to beat around the bush; I haven't got time. I like your muffins, Tanya, but I don't think I'm going to be able to keep coming here day after day with a pocket full of change. Mother Anna knows something's up. She's like a hen. She knows when she's going to lay an egg, and when she lays this one, it's going to land right on top of my head.

"Me, I'm on your side. I'm trying to help you. I'm thinking of your future. What's going to happen when you haven't got any more money coming in? I knew your mother and father, Tanya, and I'll bet they had a lot of money stashed away somewhere. Maybe it's buried in the orchard, maybe it's somewhere else. Think. Maybe you once heard them say something about it. Maybe you didn't know what they were talking about, but it stuck in your mind, and now you're big enough to put two and two together. Parents say too much in front of their kids, if you ask me. Then again, if parents always kept their mouths shut, and then they died, their kids would go hungry, right?"

All Tanya could do was look at Pavel. The sound of his voice hummed inside her head like a spinning top.

"Every cloud has a silver lining, Tanya, and all I'm asking you to do is just think about what I'm saying. Use that brain in there and try to remember where the money is, and if you have any questions, I won't steer you wrong. Understood?"

The humming stopped.

"Nobody trusts anybody anymore, Tanya, and it's a sad thing, but—what's that sound?"

Pavel tensed up to listen.

"It's the wives." He fumbled for money in his pockets. He grasped Tanya's hand, slammed coins into it, and made a dash for the birch trees.

Even as Pavel ran one way, Tanya looked across the kitchen, and through the window she saw Mother Anna and her friends coming the other way. In the barnyard the geese squawked and scattered, and there were three sharp knocks on the door. The whole door shook. Tanya was still holding the money Pavel had given her.

She dropped the coins into the pocket of her skirt and went to the door to face her visitors.

"Tanya, dear," said Mother Anna. She had a basket on her arm. One plump hand clasped the other at her waist.

"Good morning," Tanya said.

"We're starving. May we come in?"

The wives spread out in the kitchen. Their darting eyes didn't miss the broken eggshells, the open flour jar, and the jug of Milenka's milk on the counter.

"I smell muffins!" Mother Helena said.

"Yes, but"—Tanya said—"I ate them."

"Oh!" they moaned. "Please make us some."

"Do you really want me to?" Tanya said, hoping that things weren't as bad as Pavel had made them out to be.

"We have money, if that's what you mean," Mother Anna said.

"I don't mean that."

"How much?" Mother Anna said. "We don't want your charity, dear. How much?"

Tanya was dizzy with confusion. First Pavel, and now this. It was as though they were trying to catch her in a lie, but she didn't know whose lie it was.

"You don't have to pay me, Mother Anna."

"No, no, we insist. Let's say five pence for each muffin. Five pence is the going price, isn't it, ladies? We'll have a dozen muffins." Mother Anna took a purse from her basket. "A dozen muffins means each of us gets two. Two times five pence is ten pence each. Ladies?"

The arguments started. Not everyone had the right change, and they all talked at once.

"Here's a twenty-five piece, but someone's going to owe me fifteen." "I've got a fifteen piece, who's got five?" "Give her your fifteen piece and take five from—" "No, you trade your twenty-five for her fifteen, and take ten from Helena." "I put in fifteen. Somebody owes me five pence." "Who's got change for twenty?" "That's not fair. I put in twenty-five."

"All right, all right, ladies," Mother Anna said. "It'll all come out in the wash. Tanya, please make us a dozen muffins."

They sat at the table and started talking again. If someone had driven the geese in from the barnyard and chased them around the kitchen, they would have sounded like the wives talking. Tanya tried to shut her ears to all that noise and concentrate on her work.

First, she had to figure out what kind of muffins to make. There were two apples on the counter, left over from the apple cinnamon muffins she'd made for Pavel. That helped her decide.

With her little knife Tanya cut the apple into quarters and trimmed away the seeds. She put the four pieces in a row so they lay flat, and she started chopping them into tiny bits. She was doing what she loved doing. She didn't hear the wives anymore. The sunlight through the window gleamed on the knife, and the only sounds were the wet crunch of the chopping—like slicing a snowball—and the tap-tap-tapping of the blade against the counter.

But something was wrong, and when Tanya tuned her ears to the wives sitting behind her, she understood what it was. The kitchen really was quiet. The wives had stopped talking and were watching her. She missed a beat with her chopping.

"Look, ladies, it's going to be apple muffins," Mother Anna said.

"Mm!"

"Lovely!"

Tanya could have told them the recipe also called for cinnamon, but she didn't.

"Can we help?" asked Mother Anna, and they all got up and surrounded Tanya at the counter.

"Tell us what comes next." Hands reached out and grabbed the eggs and the jug of milk and the pot of butter. Mother Anna sniffed Milenka's milk.

"Do you mix the eggs and butter first, or do you put the flour in and *then* add the eggs and butter? Or do you wet the flour with milk first? Which is it? Tell us, it's so interesting."

"Well," Tanya said, "I give myself enough flour first." She turned the flour jar upside down. The flour landed in the bowl in one fat lump. "And I make sure there aren't any lumps in it." She beat the flour like mad. Clouds flew up. "This part is very important, be-cause—because—"

She threw down the biggest, wettest sneeze she could, right into the bowl.

"I'm sorry," she gasped, her face white with flour. "I got flour up my no—"

Another sneeze—another splat and spray. The wives dusted themselves off and stepped back.

"I think I'll pass, thank you."

"Let's forget the muffins, shall we?"

The trick might have worked, but Tanya had for-gotten about the coins—the money from Pavel—in her skirt pocket. The coins jingled when she sneezed. Mother Anna heard it.

Mother Anna thrust her hand into Tanya's pocket and pulled so hard, she turned the pocket inside out. The coins splattered and rolled in circles around the floor. One of them seemed to take forever to stop wob-bling and lie flat.

"Broken eggshells on the counter, and money in her pocket!"

The coins were scattered all over the floor.

"That's mine," Tanya said.

"Where did you get it?"

"I don't have to tell you."

"Don't talk to me in that tone of voice! Where did you get that money?"

"I got it from—"

"Don't lie to me, young lady!"

"Go ask Pavel!"

Mother Anna slapped her across the face.

No one had ever slapped Tanya before. Her parents had never done such a thing to her, and the surprise, the shock, hurt as much as the sting of Mother Anna's hand. Tanya touched her burning cheek. She was too startled to cry, and what happened next was so strange, she forgot to cry.

Mother Anna was doing the crying. Mother Anna's face turned red as Nikola's when he got upset, and her eyes filled with tears.

"I can't"—Mother Anna took a wadded handkerchief out of her sleeve—"I can't tell you how disappointed and hurt we are, after everything we've done for you. Didn't we try to help you when you had no one else in the world? When we found you shivering in your bed and we bathed you and dressed you in warm clothes, and fed you and took you into the bosom of our family? And to think we were all set to raise you like our own child in our own house, and love you, and protect you—and this is how you thank us!"

It must have been the slap, because Tanya had never felt so bright and alert. The words flew into her mind and out of her mouth, because they said exactly what she wanted to say.

"I didn't want your charity."

That was something Mother Anna had said earlier—

before the slap—when she insisted on paying for muffins. "We don't want your charity, dear," Mother Anna had said. Charity meant kindness. Didn't everyone want kindness? Not always. Not when it meant giving up everything in return. Tanya couldn't have put it into words, until this moment.

Mother Anna sniffled into her handkerchief. "What's wrong with our charity? What's wrong with people being kind to you? I never dreamed I'd hear such a thing. I never dreamed! Now I know we've wasted our kindness. Not a speck of gratitude! And to think her parents raised such a child."

The other wives had been looking daggers at Tanya. Now they rushed to comfort their friend.

"Don't blame the parents, Anna darling. They did the best they could."

"Everybody blames parents nowadays."

"Sure, we're always the ogres."

"You do your best and you pray your kids turn out decent, and then they break your heart."

"Just because the kids are rotten doesn't mean it's the parents' fault."

"You're so right," Mother Anna whimpered. "Let's go."

"Of course, dear heart. Let's get out of here."

"Where's my little basket?"

"It's on the table. Here, darling. And I've got our money."

"We'll sort it out later."

Suddenly Tanya felt very tired. She sat down at the table. She thought they were going to spare her any more words. She was wrong.

On their way out, Mother Anna jabbed her finger at her.

"Now you listen to me, young lady. If any of our husbands set foot in this house again, I'm holding *you* responsible!"

CHAPTER
THIRTEEN

They were banging on the door again. Tanya didn't move.

They kept banging. They weren't about to go, and the only way to make them go was to get up and answer the door.

It was a man in a weathered felt hat. His hat was spotted with old raindrops.

"Next time you powder your nose, kid, do it in front of a mirror. You want to buy a mirror?"

Tanya put her hand to her cheek, where Mother Anna's slap had left finger marks in the flour.

"Baking up a storm, huh, kid?"

"Who told you?"

"Your friend Anton the Sharpener, for one. And another guy, what's his name—Pavel. I've been hearing about you all over the place."

"I didn't do anything."

"First mistake right there. Don't ever pout. So you make muffins. Big deal. You think the world's going to beat a path to your door? You got to *sell*. Put on a show. Entertain the people. They don't pay for muffins. They pay for *you*. You're selling *you*. That's the open sesame for every wallet and purse under the sun. That's the grease on the axle of commerce. I don't care if it's dry goods, hard goods or last week's spoiled milk. You're the goods. You're the merchandise. The item. The article. The stock-in-trade. And the first rule of business is: Never turn down a sale. So don't waste my time. Show me the famous muffins."

"I don't have any."

"Didn't you hear what I just said? Money and muffins are about to change hands. You're going to make a transaction. A swap. One thing for another thing. *Quid pro quo,* that's tit for tat in Latin, and when that happens, it's beautiful, like a baby's first cry after it pops out and gets smacked on the bottom. Look into my eyes. What do you see?"

He bent down. His face was inches from Tanya's, and the eyes under the brim of his hat were cheerful and quick.

"My stomach's empty, but my pocket's full. In a minute it'll be the other way around. Can you see that? You got to learn to see that, or you'll never get anywhere in business. See it, feel it, smell it coming, like a farmer smells rain."

"You're not from our village," Tanya said.

"Mr. Ivo, traveling salesman," the man said, shaking Tanya's hand. "All manner of articles bought and sold. My money's good."

"I can't make you any muffins," Tanya said. "I don't have any more flour. I have some, but I—I sneezed into it."

"I got the perfect sneezing-and-cold remedy in the wagon. Cherry flavor. Clear your head and tickle your taste buds all at the same time. You'll like it so much, you'll want to spread it on your pancakes."

"I don't really have a cold. I was just sneezing."

"Sell you some flour, then. Better yet, if your muffins are half as good as people say they are, I'll trade flour for muffins and throw in some cash to sweeten the deal."

He walked toward the gate. Tanya watched his long-legged strides. She was so curious, she went out to the middle of the barnyard.

Through the gate she saw a wagon. It was painted dark green, like the one her parents used to have. Tanya felt a pang of joy and loss at the sight of the green wagon. She couldn't stop her eyes from looking for her parents in the front seat.

"Come on back. Show you my inventory," Mr. Ivo said.

He had pots and pans for sale and sacks of flour, rice, coffee and tea. He had tables and chairs wedged on top of each other; clocks, even a grandfather clock; oil paintings, statues, mirrors, and piles of boxes and suitcases.

"Need a hairbrush?"

One suitcase was full of brushes and combs. Another had nothing but smokers' pipes: pipes of clay, pipes carved out of the roots of trees, yellow pipes made of something that felt like hard soap, and one tall pipe with a big belly and long arms like an octopus.

"You fill it with water and five guys can puff at once. Very big in some of the villages around here. Plop the old fez on in the morning, talk about the weather between puffs, and before you know it, it's bedtime."

He slammed the suitcase shut. "You want books? Here. Life of Christ. Koran. Very interesting. Big seller. Talmud. This one goes into great detail about everything. Look at the writing. My father could read this. Books and more books. Something for everybody. Stuff for every human need. All right. Flour for the Muffin Kid."

CHAPTER
FOURTEEN

That's a tough break," Mr. Ivo said. They were in the kitchen. Tanya had washed her face, and Mr. Ivo was on his second muffin. They were talking about her parents.

"I just hope they come soon," Tanya said.

Mr. Ivo said nothing for a moment. He simply looked into Tanya's eyes.

"Yeah. But let's get back to the here and now. You've got something a lot of kids with parents don't have. You've got enterprise."

He pointed at the stack of coins on the table. They were the coins Mother Anna had torn from Tanya's pocket.

"When I was your age, I ran away from home. Hit the high road, and met some pretty low characters along the way. Food? Never saw it. Lived on dandelion salads one whole summer. Stole chickens. I could tell some stories. Some other time, maybe. But you! Here you were, by yourself, no parents, nobody. You didn't sit around and mope. You didn't go crying to the folks across the river. I like that."

Mr. Ivo rubbed his chin. His chin made a scratchy sound that reminded Tanya of her father. Whenever she heard that sound—no matter who the man was—Tanya couldn't help it, it reminded her of her father.

"Five pence per muffin," he said. Then his hand came down on the table with a bang. "Six dozen! I want six dozen muffins."

So many! Tanya was amazed. The most she'd ever made in a day was three dozen, and that was using all her muffin pans, filling them up and putting them back in the oven even before they cooled. What would Mr. Ivo do with six dozen muffins?

"I know what you're thinking," he said. "You're worried they'll go stale. I got some breadboxes in the wagon. Keep 'em fresh a thousand years."

But Tanya was still wondering why he wanted six dozen muffins. She hadn't forgotten what he'd said about running away from home and being so hungry.

"It is nice to have a snack when you're traveling," she said.

"What's that got to do with it?" he said.

"After your childhood, I'm sure you never want to go anywhere without a snack."

Mr. Ivo laughed from his gut. "You're a sweet kid! Sure, I'll save some for the road. Kid, I'm going to be your distributor. I'm going to sell your muffins along my route."

Mr. Ivo filled two of his breadboxes with warm muffins and carried them out to the wagon. They fit under the front seat.

"You're happy with the money I gave you? You counted it out?"

"Oh yes, Mr. Ivo. Thank you."

"Don't leave it lying around for somebody to steal. Hide it in a good place."

"Before you go," Tanya said, "I want you to meet someone."

"I thought you lived all alone," he said as Tanya stepped back through the gate. She swung the barn door open.

First Mr. Ivo heard the gentle hoofbeats, then out of the barn came Milenka, such a big cow with such a little girl. Tanya didn't even come up to Milenka's shoulder.

"This is my Milenka," Tanya said, laying her hand on her dusty hide. Milenka turned her head to lick Tanya's arm.

"How many quarts you get out of her?"

Tanya ran inside the barn again and came out with the milk pail. "Up to here," she pointed.

"Keep it coming." Mr. Ivo climbed into the wagon and took the reins.

"Goodbye, Mr. Ivo!" Tanya said. "I hope you sell the muffins."

"Don't worry, kid."

A shake of the reins, and the wagon lurched forward.

"Thank you again for buying them!"

"At five pence each, it was a steal."

CHAPTER
FIFTEEN

Leaning against Milenka, Tanya watched Mr. Ivo's wagon climb the rutted road along the river gorge and disappear behind the black pines. Clouds nested on the mountains. Tanya couldn't have known it then, but this was the last mild day of the season, the last of those days that come in the middle of every fall, when the dust of crumbling leaves makes a golden haze, and the summer tries to come back.

It was cooler the next day, and the sun went into hiding. Tanya was in the barnyard, feeding the chickens with corn she had gathered in the days before the weather turned. She was scraping a corncob with a knife, letting the kernels fall while the chickens nibbled around her feet. With all the clucking going on, she didn't hear anyone coming; the first thing she saw was two pairs of legs standing among the birds.

A small boy and a smaller girl were holding hands and looking at her. He wore a sheepskin jacket, and she had a babushka tied under her chin.

"Muffins for me and Sister," said the boy.

"Children? Where are you?" their mother called, as their father tied their cart horse at the gate.

The family had driven over three hills just for Tanya's muffins. Mr. Ivo had passed by their house yesterday, and the children had pleaded with their parents to take them to the Muffin Child's farm.

Tanya smiled at the children and tried to play with them, but they were shy, and looked at her, and her farm, with wide eyes.

Even in the eyes of children, the Muffin Child was different, and she lived on a farm that was different from other farms. The lost harvest and the fallen leaves made the place look savage and forgotten. Tanya had swept and cleaned around the house and the barn, but she noticed things she could do nothing about: the tumbledown fence, the broken hinge, the barn door that would have glowed with fresh red paint if her father were there, and the cobwebs in places she couldn't reach.

Those weren't the only changes the eye could see. Tanya tried to wash her skirts and sweaters and blouses, but they never came out quite as clean as when her mother used to do it for her, and she didn't have her mother to cut and brush her hair. Her hair grew out in long matted horns, and with her large watchful eyes under the tangles, she looked like a wild creature.

She looked like she belonged on that farm with its weedy barnyard, the tattered cornstalks, and the crows that flocked there under the cloudy autumn skies. No one denied that Tanya had a gift, and that her muffins were beyond compare; and it was easy to believe that her gift had left its mark on the way she looked, just as a bolt of lightning can leave its scar on a tree.

Now her customers came from farms and villages up the road, and her price jumped from five to fifteen pence. It happened like this. Mr. Ivo had turned quite a profit, charging twenty-five pence per muffin (no wonder he said five pence was a steal). So when his customers came to see Tanya, they asked her to take ten pence off his price, to make up for their traveling expenses. Tanya was glad to do it, since that still left fifteen pence for her.

Every night she counted her earnings and put them in her box, the box Mother Anna had given her, with the roses and stars on it; and every night the box went back to its hiding place under the pile of linen sheets and pillowcases in the wardrobe in her parents' room. The box was getting heavy, which meant that she would probably have enough money to tide her over once autumn slipped into winter and the cold kept people in their homes. With enough money saved up, at least she wouldn't go hungry.

No one from the village came anymore, it was as though they'd forgotten all about her; but Tanya hadn't forgotten about them. The kitchen cupboards were almost empty, and one of these days she'd have to go to the village market for food. She didn't want to go there. She didn't want to face those people. Every time she thought about it, she felt awful in the pit of her stomach.

One afternoon, she heard two people grumbling outside. She looked out the kitchen window and saw an old couple she didn't know. They weren't from the village. The husband wore a red fez and a little embroidered vest.

"Who do they think they are?" he said as he helped his wife down from their cart. "What am I, made of money?"

"Let's hope this is worth it."

Tanya went to the door to greet them.

"There she is!" the wife said as soon as she saw Tanya. "That's her."

"Can I help you?"

"You can tell your neighbors to mind their own business," the wife said.

Tanya didn't want to hear the rest, but she didn't have any choice. The husband and wife told their story together, each picking up where the other left off, as husbands and wives so often do.

"We just passed through your village and asked where to find the Muffin Child. A simple question. The minute they heard it, they were at us like hornets."

"I've never seen anything like it in my life. Worse than beggars. At least beggars beg. Those clowns acted like we owed them."

" 'Buy our wine, buy our cheese, buy our potatoes, buy this, buy that.' We don't want their junk."

"Then they tried to sell us their own muffins."

"A 'local delicacy,' they said."

"Hogwash."

"One of them grabbed our horse by the reins and tried to stop us."

"I'll tell you one thing: if they try that again on our way back, I'll run 'em over."

CHAPTER
SIXTEEN

Feeling a little *edgy* today?"

It was Anton the Sharpener, Anton with the grindstone on his back, poking his nose in the kitchen window, while Tanya sat and brooded. The old couple had just come and gone.

"Muffin, please," Anton said, and Tanya got up and served him one. But she didn't say anything and she didn't even look at him, because he reminded her too much of the village.

Anton sighed. "Yes, there's been some friction. Now that's something I know about: friction. Without friction, I'd be out of business."

"Anton, why are they being this way?"

Anton picked at his muffin. His fingers looked like a spider crawling out from under something.

"It's these muffins of yours," Anton said. "The village wives have never forgiven you for them."

"I wasn't trying to do anything bad."

"That's just it. You weren't even trying. No false starts and botched batches for you. No struggles and failures in full view of a husband. You've had it too good. It's come too easily to you. And who ever heard of a little girl selling muffins? Little girls are supposed to give their muffins away, like smiles, to make the world a sweeter place."

"I had to sell them."

"Child, you asked me why they don't like you. To begin with, you got off on the wrong foot when you ran away from Mother Anna's house."

"I didn't want to live there."

"I wouldn't want to live there either. But the fact is that you slapped Mother Anna long before she slapped you. She was trying to be nice to you, and you wouldn't let her, and she'll never forgive you for that either. People are never nice just to be nice, child. They're nice because they want to feel big. How can you feel big without someone else feeling small? You know. Small. Meek. Humble. Ever so grateful. 'Oh, thank you with all my heart,' " Anton said mockingly, forcing a feeble smile.

"Beware of nice people," he went on. "They're like money lenders. They're in it for the interest. But I wouldn't judge poor Mother Anna too harshly. Mother Anna's like most people. Most people aren't bad people. They're just, well, not so good."

"That doesn't make me bad," Tanya said.

"No," Anton said. "But people are asking questions."

"What questions?"

" 'What is she putting in those muffins? Who are those foreigners, and what are they doing milling about her house?' "

"Foreigners?"

"The couple that came looking for you today. The man wore a fez on top of his head."

"They're from another village."

"It's a good thing you live on this side of the river. You can't hear what your mother and father's old friends are saying."

"What are they saying?"

"Things like, 'Why aren't her customers our customers too? Maybe it's more than muffins they're after. Maybe they're hungry for her farm. Maybe she's going to sell it to them, and then once they get their hands on it, they'll grab another farm, and another and another, and before you know it, they'll steal the land out from under us, and drive us from our homes.' "

"I'd never sell the farm. I'm only selling muffins."

"Ah, but your muffins are the cheese that brings the rats. Don't you see?"

CHAPTER
SEVENTEEN

When Anton said those ugly words, Tanya turned her eyes away, and she found herself looking down at the windowsill, where her hands were resting.

Every year, in the spring, her father painted the windowsill white. He would stand where Anton was standing now and paint with a paintbrush made from a horse's tail. Last spring, a hair had come off the brush, and the hair had been part of the windowsill ever since. Anton's spidery fingers laid two brass coins—the money for his muffin—over that creamy white hair.

Anton walked away, leaning on his stick. Tanya put the coins in the pocket of her skirt, but she was still looking at the horsehair on the windowsill. Rain began to fall. The sun found a hole in the clouds, and the shower fell gleaming into the river gorge. Tanya searched for a rainbow but didn't see one. She gazed out at the rain for another moment and then did other things.

She washed her muffin pans and the mixing bowl, and tidied the kitchen counter. She brought some wood from the barnyard and threw it down in the alcove beside the hearth. By then she was tired and ready for a nap, but she did one last thing. She took the broom from its place in the corner and swept the kitchen floor.

As she was sweeping, the broom shed a straw. Paintbrushes and brooms, they always shed. They always left horsehairs or straws lying around. Tanya bent down, picked up the straw, and threw it in the hearth.

She couldn't have said why, but as she watched the flames eat the straw, she thought of how much her parents had taught her. They had taught her not by words but by example: by leaving little lessons lying around like the horsehair on the windowsill. They were the kind of lessons she had to learn for herself, but they weren't that hard to understand.

Again she thought of her father standing outside the window with the white-tipped brush in his hand. She remembered the sound of his voice as he would greet people who passed by the house. He would always say hello and strike up a conversation. What difference did it make whether they were neighbors and strangers? None that Tanya could ever tell.

Her mother was the same way. Almost every morning her mother would make some treat and set it aside for guests. She would make whipped cream, or a cherry tart, or pancakes so light they puffed full of air when they landed on the plate, like clean bedsheets floating down. Tanya would spend the day wishing for thunderstorms or hail or snow so people would stay in their homes and she could have her mother's treats all to herself. But she seldom got her wish. Where the guests came from was the last thing on Tanya's mind, and nothing her mother ever said to her made her think that some people were less welcome than others.

The rain was still falling. Tanya went back to the windowsill and looked down at the horsehair in the white paint. She thought of market days in the village square, she remembered how her parents would smile all day to people; and yet often on the way home, the smiles would leave her parents' faces. In the beginning, when Tanya was much younger, she used to think that her parents stopped smiling because they were angry at her for something she'd done, the mistake she'd made counting, or the eggs that had slipped from her hands. But in time she came to understand that her parents weren't angry at her; it was just the end of the day and they were by themselves again. They told her that sometimes you had to smile at people, even though you were tired or wanted to be somewhere else.

Today was market day, and Tanya had an idea. She would go to the village, buy things, and be like her parents. She would smile and show them whose daughter she was. She would make them change their minds about her.

Throwing a scarf over her head, she left the house to go to the village, with her basket on her arm.

The rain was letting up and the sun came out again. Even the weather seemed to smile back at Tanya as she jumped around the puddles in the ruts in the road. Across the river the red tiles of the village rooftops were dark and shiny in the soft light. It was such a pretty village, the way the stone houses huddled together like a flock of sheep; and the bridge leapt over the gorge like a spring lamb.

A gang of crows flew out of the gorge and left the echoes of their hoarse cries. As Tanya crossed the planks of the bridge, the river whispered to her. Then she heard something clicking. She kept going and heard the clicking again. It sounded like Nikola. She leaned out and saw him down below, almost under the bridge, playing with his blocks. He was sitting on a rocky ledge where fishermen sometimes hung their lines in the river.

"Nikola!"

Tanya let go of her basket, ran back across the bridge, and found her way down the path to Nikola. The cliff was shaggy with bushes, and she held onto them. She looked down only once. Little whirlpools were spinning like tops in the fast green water.

"Nikola, you can't stay here! You could fall."

It was damp under the bridge, and the whisper of the river rose to a shout. Nikola was banging one block against the other. Tanya stuffed the blocks into his pocket before he could start to cry.

Holding his hand, she led him up the path, away from the cliff.

"How would your momma feel if you fell in the river? Everyone would be looking for you. Your momma would cry for days. I'm bringing you back to her right now, so she won't worry about you."

They were crossing the bridge, and as Tanya picked up her basket she saw a rainbow painted on a black-and-blue cloud.

"Look at the colors, Nikola." She took his cheeks in her hands and pointed his face at the rainbow. "You should always look at rainbows. They're pretty and they don't come every day."

The rain stopped. In the village the eaves were dripping, the cobblestones black. The streets were empty, and Tanya heard the sound of wooden shutters flung back as someone opened a window. In the square the market was getting busy again after the rain shower. Down the narrow crooked street came the smell of roast chestnuts and the sellers' cries.

"Smell the chestnuts, Nikola."

There were geese and chickens and bleating goats packed together in the village square like the animals in Noah's ark. There were bakers selling loaves of braided bread, and farmers with goat cheese and sacks of flour. There were pears and grapes and greens newly washed by the rain, and carts piled with carrots and corn. People were sampling the new wine. All the smells of the market were right under Tanya's nose. A boy passed her with a catch of fish. A yellow cat, a gray cat, and a black and white cat trailed the boy, slinking between Tanya's legs and the spokes of the cart wheels. A leg of lamb smoked on a spit. A trout sizzled on a grill.

Tanya wound her way among the carts and wagons and animal pens. She was leading Nikola by the hand, looking for Mother Anna and Pavel, and she didn't see the heads turning as she passed.

"Doesn't everything smell good, Nikola? Do you see your momma and poppa?" She saw Mother Anna and Pavel across the square, Pavel with a cartload of apples and pumpkins and Mother Anna selling fruit tarts and jam. Tanya hurried toward them.

"Mother Anna, I found Nikola—"

Mother Anna was a big woman, but she bounded around the table of tarts as though she were Tanya's own size, and as light on her feet. Nikola's hand left Tanya's like a straw hat snatched by the wind. Mother Anna scooped him up and held him in her arms.

"Don't you touch my little boy!"

"I found him under the bridge," Tanya tried to explain. "He could have fallen in the river."

"The river!" someone gasped. Tanya didn't see who it was. She heard whispers around her:

"The river! That's where her parents died."

"Her poor parents, God rest their souls."

Mother Anna was kissing Nikola all over his head, but he didn't want to be kissed, and he was squirming and punching her.

"Oh, my purest sweetest adoration!" Mother Anna kissed him on the ear and the tip of his nose. "Did that girl hurt you? Did she do anything to you? Oh, my precious little innocent life, my little beating heart!"

"He was under the bridge," Tanya said, as though saying it again would clear things up. "I thought he was going to fall in the river."

"Don't you even look at him!" Mother Anna moved away, shielding Nikola's face with her fat red fingers.

There were whispers again:

"What did she say about our bridge?"

"God help us! Remember what happened to her parents?"

"Yes, remember that? We waved goodbye to them, right here in the square. They seemed perfectly fine. We all packed up our things and went home, and we never saw them again."

"How come they drowned, and she didn't?"

"What a terrible way to die! And not even a grave with their names on it."

"And then the minute they were dead, she started making those muffins."

"I never trusted that child. Ever since her parents died."

Every time someone spoke, it was as though a pair of powerful arms gripped Tanya from behind and were squeezing her tighter, making it harder and harder for her to breathe. She had to run. She knew she could breathe if she could get away. But she couldn't run in a straight line, because the square was full of people and things. She banged against the edge of a cart, slipped on the wet cobblestones, and fell.

She was sitting on the ground with her legs out in front of her, and cabbages and onions were spilling off the cart and rolling around. It was almost funny, but no one laughed. In a kind of fog, Tanya saw the shape of a man bending down to pick up an onion as it rolled toward him. It rolled right into his hand, and he threw it, and it drifted through the air and started coming down, and Tanya was wondering how it would ever land on top of the cart from which it fell; and then it hit her on the nose.

Her nose didn't start bleeding until she was on her feet and running again. The blood tasted sugary in her mouth, and everything looked smeared and jiggly and raw. She'd lost her basket in the square, and on the planks of the bridge her scarf blew away. She ran up the hill—through the puddles, splashing mud on herself—and into the cow-smelling safety of the barn.

Milenka was there. Tanya tried to put her arms around her, but she couldn't, Milenka was so big. She held Milenka's ear and the strap of her bell collar, and cried and bled on Milenka's neck. Tanya wasn't crying so much over her hurt nose, or the way the villagers had treated her. She was crying because she knew at last that her mother and father were dead.

They were dead. They had drowned. She'd heard the villagers say it. No one had ever come out and said it before. Now it was true.

She knew it was true because, in a way, she'd known it almost from the beginning, as a kind of cold frightening thought in the back of her mind. In the back of her mind was a place like the well on the farm, when you leaned over its stone rim and looked down and couldn't see anything, but you felt the chill breathing up at you. Tanya had felt the chill ever since the night the river roared over the bridge.

It was as though the river roaring over the bridge had poured into the well in the back of her mind, and she'd felt its chill ever since. But she'd tried not to shiver, and the only way to do that was to continue to believe that her parents would come back, and that they'd all be together again.

They'd never be together again—not unless she jumped in the river and drowned and the river dragged her to the bottom of the sea. She wished she were at the bottom of the sea. She wished she'd stayed on the bridge with her parents, and that the river had taken her with them.

Tanya scratched and clawed and beat Milenka with her fists. It was all Milenka's fault. Why couldn't Milenka have stayed in the barn that night? If it hadn't been for Milenka, Tanya's father wouldn't have shouted at her to jump down from the wagon and run and put Milenka inside. If it hadn't been for Milenka, Tanya would have been with her mother and father when the river roared over them; and she would be with them now, not alone in the world with a stupid cow, and nothing but enemies, and no one to help her.

CHAPTER
EIGHTEEN

She was lying on the straw, and Milenka touched her with her nose.

It was dark inside the barn. Tanya sat up. Her hand went to her mouth. Her lip was stiff and crusted. She remembered her bloody nose, remembered running home from the market. And she remembered, with shame, what she'd done to Milenka.

"Oh!"

She put her arms around Milenka's neck and kissed her and patted her where her fists had pounded and her fingers had clawed.

"I didn't mean to hurt you. I didn't mean it. I would never hurt you."

Milenka turned her head toward her, and Tanya felt her warm breath.

Was it day or night? Tanya reached down. Milenka was big with milk. It must be morning.

From the hayloft came a scratchy purring sound, a sound that Tanya had heard in past years in the barn. She felt her way to the ladder, climbed to the hayloft, and pulled open the wide door up there. It was the door her father used to pitch the hay through.

The door opened on the belly of a white fog. The gray light leaked into the back of the hayloft, where the slanting rafters met the planks of the floor. Tanya saw three tiny faces, like pale hearts sewn into a feathery quilt. They were newborn owls. They meant nothing to her.

Inside the house, Tanya looked at herself in the mirror, and she wondered who that little girl was. One nostril and her upper lip were black with dried blood. Her hair went in all directions, and had straw in it. Her eyes were red and swollen. She washed her face and did her best to get the straw out of her hair.

On the kitchen table were the last of yesterday's muffins. There were three left. On any other morning, Tanya would have thrown the stale muffins to the geese and started a fresh batch for her parents.

But she didn't make muffins this morning. Her parents were dead.

She didn't build a fire in the hearth. Her parents were dead.

She left the house, and the geese squawked and came waddling across the barnyard after her. They thought she had muffins for them. She always had muffins for them in the morning. But she went into the barn and had nothing for them. She came out of the barn with Milenka, and still had nothing for them. The geese were confused and frightened, and they squawked loudly as she went away.

Her parents were dead. The fog squatted over the countryside and blinded the sun. Tanya's hand never strayed from Milenka as they walked.

They walked down along the edge of the birch woods. They passed her father's woodpiles and the well with its pointed roof, like a witch's hat. The ground dipped, and the fallen leaves of a single great elm floated on the duck pond. The elm spread its branches into the fog. Tanya's swing hung on stiff ropes under the elm. She hadn't played on her swing in ages.

They walked to the bottom of the farm, where a ruined barn, hundreds of years old, with holes in its roof, stood back behind tall grass. The wagon ruts of an old road ran into the woods and the fog.

Crows cawed, though Tanya couldn't see them. Something was upsetting them. She leaned against Milenka for a time, stroking her, looking toward the house.

Then they walked back. They passed the oak tree

again. The house and the barn crawled out of the fog. Tanya didn't see anyone. But she heard someone banging around inside the kitchen.

A plate crashed. Tanya ran inside.

A huge crow was pecking at one of yesterday's stale muffins. The glossy black wings were spread in the air, and the claws gripped the table. The muffin plate lay in pieces on the floor.

"Who said you could eat my muffins?" Tanya shouted.

The crow cawed. The caw was so loud in the kitchen, it hurt Tanya's ears.

"Go away, crow!"

Tanya grabbed the broom from the corner and chased the crow out the door. The bird flew with the muffin in its beak. It perched in the barnyard, clutching the slanting roof over the woodpile there. Tanya swung the broom.

"Put that muffin down!"

With another loud caw, the crow dropped the muffin and flew up into the fog. Now the geese attacked the muffin. Over their squawking, Tanya looked around and wondered where Milenka was.

"Milenka?"

The broom fell from Tanya's hand. Her quick feet carried her out over the wet grass and leaves. Her eyes tried to pierce the fog.

"Milenka?"

Crows answered in the distance. Tanya could barely see to the well.

"Milenka!"

Milenka was near the well, staring, the way she stared at strangers on the farm.

"Milenka, what is it?"

She went to Milenka, and touched her.

"Milenka, what do you see?"

A sound came out of the earth, the sound of something plunking down in the well. Tanya saw a movement. Someone was at the well.

"Who are you?" Tanya said.

The figure moved. It was an old woman, tall, with a slight stoop and hair the color of the fog. Her hair was parted in the middle, with two thick braids hanging down past her waist. Her skirt was red, green and black. It dragged on the grass and leaves.

"Who are you?" Tanya's throat clicked with fright.

"Vrana," the old woman said, in the voice of a crow, if a crow could take human form.

A crow answered from the orchard. Tanya knew that voice. It was the crow she'd chased from the kitchen.

Out of the fog the crow came flapping, enormous and black. It cupped its wings to slow its flight and landed on the old woman's shoulder, like a pet.

"Vrana," the old woman said softly to the crow.

Milenka sniffed the grass at Tanya's feet.

The old woman said something: strange words. Milenka's bell clanked as she looked up.

The old woman said something else, and Tanya felt Milenka's great ribs slide away under her hand, and then her hand had nothing to rest on. Milenka wasn't standing next to her anymore, but had moved forward.

"Milenka!" Tanya whispered. "Where are you going?"

Milenka dipped her head like a puppy. She was still looking at the old woman.

"Milenka!" Tanya said. "Listen to me when I talk to you."

But Milenka was listening to the old woman. The old woman was talking to Milenka, talking in a language Tanya couldn't understand. Milenka flicked her tail.

"Milenka, back to the barn right now!" Tanya pulled Milenka's tail. "Milenka!"

Milenka snorted, and the woman chuckled.

The crow took flight and cawed, and the old woman turned and walked away, her skirt brushing the ground. The fog swallowed her up, and Vrana's calls echoed up the hill.

"Milenka!" Tanya ran around in front of Milenka and shook her finger at her. "Don't you ever listen to anyone but me again!"

Milenka licked Tanya's finger as if nothing had happened—as if the old woman had cast a spell, and Milenka didn't remember a thing. Tanya took Milenka by her bell collar, shut her inside the barn, and ran into the house to huddle at the hearth.

She dumped the last of the dry leaves out of the basket, broke twigs, and set the kindling aflame. She laid logs on the fresh fire, one neatly after the other. Her hands did all the work, and her mind was going elsewhere. Who was that old woman? What was she doing at the well? What was she saying to Milenka? What if she came back, and took Milenka away with her? The fears and questions flared up in Tanya's mind like the flames before her eyes.

The traces of the crow—the broken plate and the other muffins—were lying on the floor, and Tanya couldn't bear the sight of them. She threw the muffins out the door and heard the squawking of the geese. She reached for the broom to sweep up the mess, but the broom was where she'd left it, in the barnyard.

As she went out to pick up the broom, two crows swooped down and fought the geese for the muffins.

"Go away!" Tanya swept the crows off their feet. But she didn't see the squat little man who entered by the gate, slipped his shotgun from his shoulder, and fired.

The blast tore bits of thatch off the roof of the house. Tanya dropped the broom and covered her head. Another blast filled the air with crows flying for their lives.

"Scarecrows, forget it," the little man said. "They're wise to that."

He wore a filthy sheepskin vest and a hat missing half a brim, and he was greasy and hadn't shaved in a while.

"You frightened me," Tanya said. "Who are you?"

"I'm Zabit. Why? You heard of me?"

"No."

Zabit cracked his gun open and let the paper shells drop to the ground. A rooster pecked at one of them and twitched in disgust.

"So give me a muffin," Zabit said. "You think I came here to shoot crows?"

"I'll have to make you some," Tanya said.

"That's how it works, huh?"

Tanya was going to sweep the kitchen floor, but Zabit changed her mind for the time being. He tracked mud in and stepped on the broken pieces of the plate, breaking them into more pieces.

"You and my wife are two of a kind," Zabit said, shoving the pieces out of his way with the muddy toe of his boot. "Temper tantrums. Every time my wife gets a temper tantrum, you can kiss the plates goodbye. Smashes every plate in the house. We eat out of wooden bowls now."

"A crow did that," Tanya said. "I hate crows."

He sat at the table while Tanya cracked an egg over

flour in the bowl. He didn't know what to do with him-self, so he fidgeted and squinted out the window every time a crow cawed.

"I'm hungry," Zabit said. "I came a long way to get here. And I still got a long way to go."

"Where are you from, Zabit?"

"From up that way," he said, pointing up the road with this thumb.

"What village?"

"You couldn't call it a village. You could call it a house."

"In the mountains?"

"You could say so. Nice, quiet area. Nobody bothers you. Good place. No need to look over your shoulder when it's time to pee. It's just you and the sheep."

Zabit sent a gob of spit out the window.

"I'm headed down that way. You know the people in the village down there?"

"Yes."

"They friendly?"

Tanya didn't say anything.

"Fine with me. I got my gun. Just in case we don't see eye to eye. You never know. We might have a slight difference of opinion."

Tanya wasn't paying much attention to Zabit any-more. She was stirring batter in the bowl.

"So the neighbors aren't friendly, huh? Doesn't

bother me. I got my gun. How about the Gypsies? You had any trouble with them?"

Tanya stopped what she was doing. "What Gypsies?"

"The Gypsies in your meadow."

CHAPTER

NINETEEN

I said, up in your meadow. How long they been there?"

The bowl almost slipped from Tanya's arms. She put it down.

"What's the matter with you?" Zabit said.

"I think I saw one of those Gypsies," she said, steadying herself against the counter.

"Yeah, they're up in your meadow. I saw the wagons. You didn't know? Bet they came last night. That's when they like to travel. At night, or when it's foggy, like today."

Zabit said nothing more, and Tanya was too troubled to speak. She put a muffin pan in the oven, then stood with her arms crossed, clutching herself, in front of the fire.

"When will the Gypsies be leaving?"

"How should I know?" Zabit said. "They could be gone tomorrow morning. They could be there until spring. They come, they go, they do what they want. I wonder if they're the same ones we had in the mountains."

"You had Gypsies?"

"We had Gypsies. We had a lot of sick and dead animals, with those Gypsies."

"What do you mean?" Tanya said, turning to face Zabit.

"I mean we had a lot of sick and dead animals. Gypsies know how to make animals sick. Then they come to you and say they'll cure them—for a price. If they don't think you've paid them enough, the animal dies. The muffins are ready. I can smell them. What are you gawking at me for? I said the muffins are ready."

Another minute, and the muffins would have burned. Zabit looked up at Tanya as she served him.

"Your face is all red. You shouldn't stand so close to the fire. It's bad for you."

Zabit was on his second muffin when Tanya asked him if Gypsies could talk to animals.

"Yes!" Zabit bobbed his head up and down. "One time I saw a Gypsy with a bear. He had the bear on a chain. The Gypsy was beating a drum, and the bear was standing up on its hind legs and dancing, like this." Zabit did a bear's wobbly dance, shuffling in the firelight in his sheepskin vest and muddy boots, holding his hands out like claws, and grabbed another muffin from the table.

"Hide your money, those Gypsies'll steal it!" were his parting words. He wiped his face in the drizzle, spat, and walked out the gate, rolling his burly shoulders like a bear. Tanya came within a breath of asking him to stay. She didn't like him very much, but he had a gun, and he could shoot it—like he shot at the crows—if the old Gypsy came back to steal Milenka.

But Zabit was gone, and it rained hard again. The kitchen grew dark around the glowing hearth.

Only once before, and only for a moment, had Tanya ever seen Gypsies. Two summers earlier, beetles had attacked the crops, and the farmers had gone around to each others' farms to gather up and destroy as many of the beetles as they could. The farmers had come to help Tanya's father that day, and they were making a fire of the beetles. Tanya saw it. It was happening behind the barn, in the burning pit, a shallow hole in the ground where her father burned old hay and garbage.

It was an awful sight, that burning of the beetles; and the only thing that made it any better was knowing that the beetles were pests and everyone would be happier without them. The farmers dumped baskets full of beetles into the burning pit and stood around with rakes, making sure all the beetles burned. The beetles smoked like a pile of wet leaves. The ones on the edge of the flames crackled, and some were buzzing their brittle wings, trying to fly away.

Then the breeze turned, and the smoke blew in Tanya's face. She coughed, felt sick, and drifted over to the wall overlooking the road.

The wall was just a long heap of stones, and you didn't have to be big to see over it. Three wagons rattled past, and Tanya had a glimpse of thin children in ragged clothes, with dark skins, and burning eyes looking out under masses of black hair. The wagon wheels were painted red. There were pots clattering against the sides of the wagons, and long strings of garlic bulbs shaking. In the last of the wagons a woman sat with a long skirt trailing down. She held a baby to her breast.

Around the beetle fire the men were scowling in the heat. They turned their necks to follow the dusty wake of the three wagons.

"Gypsies," someone said.

She ran to the house to tell her mother.

"Momma, Momma, I saw Gypsies!"

"I saw them go by," her mother said.

In those days the kitchen counter came up to Tanya's eyes. Her mother's shiny creased hands were inches away, peeling garlic bulbs. Tanya was looking at her mother's familiar hands, but thinking of the garlic dangling from the Gypsy wagons.

"They're poor people," Tanya said.

"They want us to think they're poor people," her mother said. "But they have gold."

Then her mother said: "They steal."

All that rainy day after Zabit left, Tanya kept Milenka inside the barn, and went three times to see if she was all right.

Late in the afternoon, she went timidly to the well. The rain had washed the fog just a little. She could see her swing hanging from the elm tree, the scraggly orchard and the rotten cornstalks, bent and brown. She stood blinking in the rain. She saw no one.

The well on Tanya's farm had a cart wheel mounted under the little roof, and around the axle, the bucket rope was coiled. Tanya turned the cart wheel to lower the bucket. The well breathed up at her from out of its cold throat. She heard the plunk of the bucket down in that darkness full of watery echoes, and it startled her.

Even when she tried not to think about the Gypsies, they were there, like a toothache. That night, lying in bed listening to the rain, she kept hearing strange sounds outside, and she thought she heard Milenka's voice. Tanya took two pillows, bundled up two quilts, shoved her bare feet into shoes, and ran across the barnyard in her nightshirt, to spend the night in the barn, and watch over Milenka.

"Milenka, it's me."

There was a lantern on a shelf to the right of the

door, together with a box of matches. Tanya lit the lantern. It threw wild shadows. She held it high, searching every nook of the barn. The geese and chickens were nestled in sleep. In her stall, Milenka sniffed Tanya's hand, and she was sure Milenka was wondering why she had come, so many hours before dawn.

"I'm staying here with you," Tanya said, stroking her. "I want you to tell me if you hear anything. I'll be upstairs, Milenka. I'll see you in the morning." Tanya didn't want to frighten Milenka, or mention the old Gypsy woman, or say anything about Gypsies.

Her father had always told her to be careful with the lantern inside the barn. She left the lantern on the ground before climbing the ladder to the hayloft. There were cracks between the planks of the hayloft, and the lantern, shining up through the cracks, painted the rafters with golden stripes. The light was just enough for Tanya to find a good place to put her pillows and quilts on a bed of hay, not too close to the owls' nest.

Many times in the past, Tanya had begged her mother and father to let her sleep in the barn as an adventure. Now she got her wish. The lantern flickered out down below, and the stripes on the rafters faded to black. She didn't mind being up in the hayloft in the dark. It was a comfort to spend the night with the animals, to know they were there, and to hear them move about. She lay on her side, cozy in her quilts, with the hay bunched up around her. She tried to fall asleep. The rain rumbled softly on the thatch roof. Sometimes she heard the stirrings of the owl children on the other side of the hayloft.

Her eyes opened wide. She remembered the box with all her money in it: the box under the linen sheets and pillowcases in the wardrobe in her parents' room, in the house.

"Hide your money!" Zabit had said. What if the Gypsies went into the house? Her parents' room would be the first place they looked for something to steal. Tanya shut her eyes and tucked the quilts tighter under her chin. But she kept seeing ragged Gypsies—like mice in the dark, sniffing for food—creeping up the stairs, opening the wardrobe, feeling under those linen sheets and pillowcases. What would she do without money?

The minutes passed with the rain rumbling above her head, and Tanya knew she'd never fall asleep as long as that box remained where it was. She knew what she had to do, but it took her a little longer to work up the courage to do it.

She climbed down the ladder. She didn't light the lantern, because she didn't want any Gypsies to see her going back into the house. She put her shoes on and dashed across the barnyard. She shut the house door behind her. There was a hint of red in the dark of the kitchen, from the embers in the hearth. She paused and listened to the house. Her mouth was open and she held her breath, and her heartbeat was knocking inside her throat. She tiptoed up the stairs to her parents' room. Her hand felt the cold flank of the wardrobe and then the knobs on its doors. The doors opened to the fading smell of lavender. Her hands moved down the folds of linen sheets, came to the wood of the shelf, and she reached in and felt the square edge of the box under the weight of the sheets. The box was still there, heavy with coins sliding back and forth.

Downstairs at the front door, she looked outside before running back across the barnyard. If anyone was out there, they were hiding from the rain. The barnyard was one big puddle, jumping with raindrops. Tanya wasn't halfway across it when she wished she'd brought a pair of dry socks and a towel with her. Her shoelaces weren't tied, and her left shoe came off. She shoved her toes back into it and fled inside the barn.

Milenka was sleeping in her stall, her breathing almost silent. Tanya left her wet shoes under the ladder to the hayloft. She climbed up, wrapped her quilts around her, and rubbed her feet together like sticks to make fire.

CHAPTER
TWENTY

In the middle of the night, Tanya woke up to see if her box was still there, next to her. It was. Then she called out:

"Milenka! Milenka!"

From Milenka's stall came the clank of her bell.

"Nothing," Tanya said. "Go back to sleep."

She was wakened in the morning by the shouts of crows on the roof and by the thumping of their claws as they hopped about on the thatch. The rain had stopped. The first thing Tanya did was put her box in a safe place in the hayloft. She found a narrow space between an oak timber and the stone wall at the back of the barn. She put the box there, on its side, and shoved some hay in front of it. To help herself remember where it was, she counted the timbers on her fingers, up to the front of the barn. She counted ten timbers. Her box was hidden behind the tenth timber from the front of the barn.

She milked Milenka and carried the pail of milk into the house. In the kitchen she made a fire and put her shoes to dry on the stone curb around the hearth. They were still wet from last night.

Then, as she was about to go upstairs to get dry socks, she noticed the mud on the floor.

Someone had been in the house during the night and had left his dirty signature. The mud tracks started at the door and went upstairs. The mud was dry by now, and it crumbled under her bare feet. It led right to her parents' room, right to the wardrobe. Tanya flung the doors open, dreading to see the linens and pillow-cases in disarray.

But the linens were as neat as always. The muddy trail was from Tanya herself the night before, when she came to get her box.

She let out a groan and flopped down on the bed. Her little body shook with dry sobs and weak laughter, because she felt silly, miserable, and at her wits' end, all at the same time.

Someone banged on the door downstairs.

"Tanya!"

Tanya sat up on the bed.

"Tanya, it's Pavel! Listen to me! I'm sorry about what happened at the market the other day. I didn't have anything to do with it."

She didn't move. She could hear his voice coming from downstairs. He was leaning against the door, talking through the crack. He was being polite all of a sudden, not barging in, the way he usually did.

"Oh, come on," he said. "I have something to tell you."

Pavel didn't know she was upstairs. He sounded stupid, talking through the crack in the door.

"Tanya, I'm your friend."

Kneeling on the pillows, Tanya reached up and pulled the iron latch to open the window.

"Who threw that onion at me?"

"Not me," Pavel said.

"Then who did?"

"Somebody else. Forget it. Tanya, Gypsies! Gypsies in your meadow!"

"I know," Tanya said.

"Did you see what they did to your orchard?"

"Why don't you just tell me, instead of getting me all excited?"

"You won't believe me if I tell you. Come and I'll show you."

Tanya wondered what Pavel had up his sleeve. She didn't want to go with him. Then she changed her mind. She knew she'd have to go look sooner or later, and if she ran into Gypsies, it would be better to have someone with her, even if it was Pavel.

"All right, but you'll have to wait while I put my

socks on," Tanya said, and pushed the window shut. She went into her room, put her cold feet in warm socks, and got dressed: first a cotton teddy, then a woolen skirt and sweater. She tried to brush her hair (there was straw in it) but her hair was too tangled. She laced up a pair of boots—didn't get the laces right in all the little hooks—wrapped her neck in a scarf, and went out to meet Pavel.

"Who told you about the Gypsies?" Pavel said, breaking into a fast walk to the orchard. Tanya could barely keep up with him.

"Someone," she said.

"Who?"

"A man who came yesterday."

"Somebody from around here?"

"No, from up the road."

"What was his name?"

"Zabit."

"Zabit who?"

"I don't know, just Zabit."

"What'd he look like?"

"I don't remember."

"He sounds like a shady character. We don't need any more shady characters around here," Pavel said.

The fog had blown away, and the wind tore the rainclouds to rags. Tanya and Pavel turned the corner around the barn. Their eyes climbed the hill, searching for the Gypsy wagons.

"You can't see them from here," Pavel said. "They're in the meadow, way back by the edge of the forest."

Tanya knew exactly where the wagons were. They were up behind the curve of the hill, where the meadow met the black pines: where she used to walk Milenka, and let the wind lift her mind like a leaf and carry it over the valleys studded with haystacks, out over the sea.

The wind scattered the fallen leaves as Tanya and Pavel stepped over to the orchard. "Look!" he said, pointing to the nearest tree.

There, between the knuckles of the roots, a fresh hole smelled of wet earth. Someone had come during the night and dug a hole a foot deep, throwing the lumps of earth to either side.

"Look over there!" Pavel said. There was another hole under the next tree.

"They're all over the place!" he said, with a sweep of his arms.

Almost every tree had a hole under it, and the lumps of earth were strewn about. Tanya ran through the windy orchard. Whoever had done this, didn't even have pity on the trees. You could see the white flesh of the roots where the shovel had cut them.

"Money!" Pavel shouted after her. "They were looking for money! That's what you get for letting Gypsies in!"

"I didn't let them in!"

"You did!"

The wind blew Tanya's hair in her face, but she didn't do anything about it. She shambled down the orchard, not daring to lift her eyes to look at those poor trees her father had tended so lovingly. Pavel kept shouting at her.

"Look at this orchard! Look at that field! The place looks like a jungle. Like nobody's lived here for a hundred years. Out of all the farms around here, why do you think the Gypsies picked this one? Because they knew they could get away with it. They knew nobody cared."

By now, Pavel had dropped his voice. He wasn't shouting any longer. But he was still saying things Tanya didn't want to hear.

"Remember the harvest? Remember when we asked you to let us work on this farm? You said no. Well, now look at it. This was once a beautiful farm! And now you've got Gypsies. Serves you right."

"How could they do it?" Tanya said, wiping her eye.

"They're Gypsies," Pavel said.

The next thing Pavel said made Tanya think of Vrana and the old woman.

"The Gypsies came because the crows were here. Birds of a feather. They followed the crows, that's what they did."

Pavel looked once around the orchard—at the torn

earth and the mush of rotten apples on the ground—
and then at Tanya.

"Did they take your money?"

"What?" Tanya said. She was still thinking of the
old woman whispering to the crow on her shoulder, and
the crow flapping its wings.

"Did they find your money? Did you have money
buried?"

"No." Tanya shook her head and leaned wearily
against a tree. The naked branches clacked together in
the wind, like claws.

"Tanya!" Pavel whispered as he crouched down.
Now he was looking up at her. His moustache twitched
as his mouth moved. "Tanya, I know people haven't
been very friendly lately. I think it's all one big misun-
derstanding, and that's what I've been telling people.
I've been defending you. I'm on your side. The people
in our village aren't so bad. They say things and they
don't even know what they're saying. You have to be
patient with them. Especially now, with those Gypsies
around. You need to know who your friends are. Who
can you trust, if you can't trust your own people?
What's going to happen when the Gypsies break into
your house in the middle of the night? What are you
going to do?"

"I don't know," Tanya said.

"The least you can do is put your valuables in a safe

place. Are you listening to me? What about your parents' money? We talked about that before, remember? It's hidden somewhere. It's got to be. Did you ever find it?"

"No."

"Then you'd better start looking, because if you don't find it, the Gypsies will. They can tell where there's buried treasure. They know how to find metal under the ground. They have ways."

Crouching beside Tanya, Pavel was pulling up blades of grass and twisting them around his finger.

"What about all the money you've made from your muffins? I bet you've got a nice piece of change piled up by now."

"No," Tanya said.

Pavel threw away the grass with an angry flick. "No? What do you mean, No?"

"It's not as much as you think," Tanya said.

"How much is it?"

"I don't know. I've been spending it," Tanya said.

"Spending it on what?"

"On flour, and sugar, and my own food."

"You haven't been spending it at the village market. We've hardly seen you except the other day, and you weren't there two minutes."

"I've been buying things from the other people."

"You mean those foreigners from the other villages?"

"Yes."

Pavel was taken aback, and Tanya could see the suspicion in his eyes. He couldn't make up his mind whether or not to believe her. She was glad she'd lied about her customers, because Pavel didn't know them, and couldn't check her story.

"Well, if you've been buying from *them*," he said, standing up, "you haven't been getting our low prices."

He stood with his hands in his pockets, debating within himself what to do next.

"I haven't had any breakfast," Pavel said. "Why don't you make me some muffins?"

"What if Mother Anna finds out?" Tanya replied, just to needle him, to get back at him for all his questions.

"Keep Mother Anna out of this, will you?"

"I won't tell!" Tanya said.

But Pavel wasn't in a mood for jokes, and as they left the orchard, he said:

"You shouldn't be so hard on Mother Anna. She likes you. She does. She told me. Anyway, you don't know her like I do. That woman's got a heart that's just too big for one human being, that's all I can say. The way she is with our little Nikola, always fussing and fretting over him, it'd tear you apart to see it. All right, I admit, she's a little jealous because your muffins are so good. So what? It doesn't mean anything."

They went to the house. Tanya saw Pavel's eyes slide along under his lids as he glanced out toward the gate. He still didn't want to be seen with her.

The smell of burning leather stung Tanya's nose the moment they entered. She'd forgotten about her shoes drying in front of the fire.

She jumped to pluck the shoes away, trying not to scorch her fingertips. The shoes landed on the floor.

"You're giving me ideas," Pavel said. "Mind if I dry my shoes? I put a pair of clean socks on this morning, but my shoes are all wet. I was out in the rain last night."

"What were you doing?" Tanya asked, just to make conversation. It wasn't until after she'd spoken that she knew why she'd asked the question.

Pavel didn't answer at first, but sat down and unlaced his shoes. He pulled his shoes off and said: "Oh, helping somebody out. I'm trying to make some extra money."

He set his shoes on the stone curb of the hearth, then put his feet up on the table, wiggling his toes in his socks. Tanya started on the muffins. It gave her time to think about the orchard, and about everything that Pavel had said.

"Pavel, how did you find out about the holes in the orchard?"

Pavel's arms were folded on his chest. He seemed to be dozing off by the fire. "Hm?" he said, opening his eyes. "I was on my way to my field this morning and I looked. I always look at that orchard when I go by. I'm a farmer, remember? When I see a beautiful orchard going to waste, it breaks my heart. So I peeked over the wall."

"Oh," Tanya said. But she still didn't know whether to believe him.

"Gypsies made those holes," Pavel said. "They went in there with a shovel and ripped the orchard apart. All those cuts in the roots? No farmer would do that. Only a Gypsy would commit such a crime. They were looking for money! That's all there is to it," he said, and closed his eyes again.

The muffins were cooking and Pavel started to snore. Tanya freshened the fire in the hearth. Then her hands went to Pavel's empty shoes, which she moved a little to help them dry more evenly. She did this without thinking. It was the kind of thing she would have done to her own shoes lying there to dry. But when she saw the apple skin stuck to the bottom of Pavel's right shoe, and the red mush on the sole of his other shoe, her mind ran away on her.

Pavel did it. Pavel was in the orchard last night, and the proof was on his shoes. Tanya looked to see if he was watching her. His cap was pulled down over his eyes and his chin was buried in the rolled neck of his sweater. She stepped back toward the oven, behind him.

She couldn't keep still. She covered her mouth with her hands, bit her thumbnail, and paced back and forth in the beam of sunlight slanting through the window. Pavel was the one. Pavel had dug the holes in the orchard and blamed it on the Gypsies. Why? To frighten her, and to make her tell him where her money was, so he could steal it.

For a while, Tanya knew she was right. But then she looked across the kitchen to the muddy trail up the stairs. She remembered how sure she'd been that those footprints told an intruder's tale. Maybe she was just as wrong about Pavel's shoes. The shoes didn't prove anything. Pavel didn't have to go to her orchard to step on apples. He had his own orchard. There were apples on the ground everywhere. It was the season.

Her nose told her the muffins were ready. At least she wasn't wrong about that. She took them out of the oven and said:

"Pavel. Muffins."

Pavel scratched the back of his head, dropped his feet to the floor, and bent over his breakfast.

"Mm," he mumbled. "Best muffin I ever had. Make me some tea, will you?"

His eyes were on Tanya as she went to put the kettle on the hearth.

"Those Gypsies are going to be a problem for all of us," Pavel said. "People are going to be afraid to go out at night from now on. You know who's going to get rich from this whole thing? The locksmith. People are going to be putting locks on their houses and barns."

"Their barns?" Tanya said.

"Suppose your cow got sick and looked like it was going to die. Wouldn't you pay somebody to cure it? That's a Gypsy trick. They know all the poisons, all the weeds and mushrooms. But for every poison there's always some berry or piece of bark or something that works against the poison, and the Gypsies have that up their sleeve. So they'll slip the poison to an animal when you're not looking, and then make you pay an arm and a leg to save the animal. Every time somebody's animal gets sick, there's always some Gypsy around to help out. But Gypsies aren't the cure. They're the disease."

"Can they talk to animals?"

He helped himself to another muffin. "A lot of people say that, but I don't believe it. Gypsies don't have any special powers. It's all tricks. People say Gypsies can see the future in the palm of your hand. Nonsense! You can't see the future in somebody's hand. Look! You see my hand?"

Pavel showed Tanya his hand. She was pouring his tea into a mug.

"See these callouses? That one's my field. This here's my orchard, there's my woodpile, and all these scars and wrinkles are my hard work, dawn till dusk, day after day, ever since I was a kid. End of story. I don't need a Gypsy to tell me that. But people will believe anything. They always want to know the future! What's going to happen to me tomorrow, and the day after that, and the day after that? Am I going to get rich? Are my children going to make me proud? Are things going to get any better, or are they just going to stay the same?"

"I wish I knew the future," Tanya said.

"No, you don't. You don't want to know anything about the future. When you were just a carefree little kid running around this farm, would you have wanted to know your parents were going to die on you? Believe me, ignorance is bliss. Look at me and Mother Anna. You think we'd have wanted to know about our little Nikola—"

For a moment Pavel couldn't go on. His throat tightened, and his eyes sparkled with tears.

"Our little Nikola," he said a second time, under his breath. His moustache quivered. He cleared his throat and took a noisy slurp of tea.

"Is something wrong with Nikola?" Tanya said, thinking that maybe Nikola was sick, or had fallen and hurt himself.

"Is something wrong with him? Of course something's wrong with him. He never says anything. He never looks at anybody. He plays with those blocks all day long, click clack, click clack, I'm sick of listening to it. Click clack, click clack, like a voice yelling at me:

'This is what you've got for a son, this is what you've got for a son.' Sometimes I want to take those blocks in my hands and crush them to sawdust! Give me more tea."

He swallowed more tea.

"We used to say, 'Whatever's wrong with him, he'll grow out of it.' He's not going to grow out of it. He'll be an idiot all his life, you hear me? An idiot! And how's that going to make me look?"

Tanya could never say she trusted Pavel, but there was nothing false about the way he was speaking now.

"You should see what it's doing to Mother Anna," Pavel said. "Nikola, Nikola, Nikola, that's all she ever thinks about. She loves him ten times more than all our other kids put together. And no matter how bad he gets, when he screams and breaks things, she won't even shake her finger at him. Me, sometimes I want to grab him and yell: 'Stop this! Why can't you be like other kids?' I tell you, if I ever did that, I swear to God, Mother Anna'd smash my head like a pumpkin and throw me in the river."

Pavel shook his head. "Mothers and their children. What was God thinking when He made us this way?"

He looked over at Tanya, as if he'd just remembered she was listening to him.

"I bet you think I'm some kind of weakling, coming and crying to you. You don't even know what I'm talking about. Well, someday when you have kids of your own and something bad happens to them, you'll know what I'm going through."

Tanya almost said what she was thinking: that she understood very well how he felt. An orphan could understand anything.

"I don't know what to do," Pavel said. He started on his third muffin. "We heard there's some big doctor in the capital who can maybe help our little Nikola. But we'd have to go there. The whole family, stay in some hotel and pay through the nose just to live there while we try to get in to see this doctor. But if I thought he could make our little guy into a normal kid, it'd be worth it, just to see Mother Anna smile at her beautiful boy. That's why I was out last night, trying to dig up some money. I need money. I don't care how I get it."

One moment, Tanya was feeling sorry for Pavel; the next, she suspected him again. She imagined him in the orchard, in the rain, gripping a shovel. She heard the shovel sinking into the ground while he stepped on soggy apples—

Pavel jumped up like a Jack-in-the-box.

"Get out of here!" he roared.

Three children—two boys and a girl—ran from the window. Tanya heard the scrambling of their feet and the geese squawking in the barnyard. Pavel opened the door and looked out. The children were over by the barn, waiting for Pavel's next move. They looked like wet birds. They were Gypsies. The girl wore a long skirt and her hair fell in her face.

"I said get out of here!"

The little Gypsies answered Pavel at once, but without a word.

The girl stuck out her tongue.

One boy put his thumb to his nose and twinkled his fingers.

The other boy did something with his arm. Tanya didn't know what it was supposed to mean, but it was like a hoe popping up when you step on it.

"I'll murder you!" Red in the face, Pavel lurched toward the hearth and stumbled into his shoes. But the children were faster, and before he was out the door they were out of the barnyard. They kept running, past the well to the bottom of the orchard. Tanya trotted out behind Pavel.

"Get lost!"

Fleeing up the orchard, the three taunted him again and called out to him in their Gypsy language.

"That's what makes me so mad," Pavel said through his teeth. "Healthy kids like that, and then I look at our little Nikola."

He swung around and cried out at Tanya: "How come those Gypsy kids are all right? Why aren't their parents sobbing over them? What did I do to deserve a son like mine?"

He looked into Tanya's face and saw that it had no answers for him, and he bent down to tie his shoelaces.

"I'm late. I've got to go."

Pavel stuck his hands in his pockets and walked away, back to the barnyard and out of sight. He didn't offer to pay for his muffins, and after hearing him talk so much about needing money, Tanya didn't mention it.

She looked up at the orchard. The rows of apple trees without their leaves looked like spiders with their legs in the air. The earth was torn up and full of holes.

Maybe the Gypsies were the culprits, just as Pavel said. Didn't Gypsies do those kinds of things? Hadn't her mother said so?

"They steal," her mother had said.

"Who can you trust," Pavel had said, "if you can't trust your own people?" Whom could Tanya trust, if not her own mother? Her mother had never lied to her. But her mother wasn't around to tell her the truth anymore. Her mother had never lived to see the orchard like this, torn up and fallen into ruin.

The wind blew through the orchard and scattered the leaves for the thousandth time, and Tanya pressed her hands to her head to keep it from bursting: bursting with all these things she'd never had to think about before, all these questions she'd never had to ask.

CHAPTER
TWENTY-ONE

Late that afternoon, Tanya raked the dirty hay from the floor of the barn. It gave her something to do while she watched over Milenka. She raked the hay into one pile, opened the barn's back door, and raked the pile of hay out to the burning pit. The hay burned bright in the dusk. Tanya stood by the fire and looked for Gypsies. Along the hilltops, the bare trees bristled against the gray sky.

When the fire burned out, she climbed the ladder to the hayloft to get clean hay. She gathered the hay in her arms and threw it down below, then spread it inside Milenka's stall, the chicken coop, and the pen where the geese slept.

It was tiring work, and she was almost too tired to make herself supper that evening. She ate beans and cabbage by the lights of the hearth and a candle. She was having bread with her meal when she saw spots of mold on the loaf. She gave up on supper. She wasn't that hungry anyway.

The feather of flame on the end of the candle became two feathers, shining side by side . . . Tanya lifted her head. She'd fallen asleep at the table. The fire in the hearth had dwindled to embers, and the candle flame struggled to keep from drowning in its tiny lake of wax. It was late, time to be in the barn with Milenka.

The flame spun yellow webs in Tanya's eyelashes as she went upstairs holding the candle. She got her nightshirt and pulled the quilt off her parents' bed. She would change her clothes in the barn. Starting tomorrow, she told herself, she would have to think about what else to bring to the hayloft, now that it was going to be her bedroom. She blew out the candle, shut the door to the house, and crossed the barnyard under a sprinkling of stars. She opened the barn door and felt a draft of cold air from inside.

She'd left the back door of the barn open. It had been open all this time, all through supper, ever since she'd finished with the hay.

"Milenka?" Tanya dropped her bundle and ran inside. She couldn't see into the dark of Milenka's stall, but she didn't need the lantern to see that Milenka was gone.

How could she have let it happen? How could she have thrown the hay in Milenka's stall, said goodbye to her, hung the rake and the pitchfork on the wall, and closed the front door, without even a glance toward the back of the barn? She'd felt tired and lonely—but how could she have been so stupid?

She ran the length of the barn and out to the burning pit. It still smelled of warm ashes. She stood banging her fists against her hips, furious with herself, and frightened.

"Milenka!"

The half moon lay on its back. Tanya looked for the moonlight to pick Milenka's white spots out of the dark. Sometimes Milenka wandered up the orchard. There Tanya searched. She tripped over a root, and her foot went down into one of the holes and she toppled forward, breaking her fall with her hands. The skin of a rotten apple burst between her fingers.

Milenka wasn't in the orchard. Tanya turned back. The night was very still. She heard herself panting, heard the thump of her footsteps, and then each time she stopped, she heard the echo of her voice calling out for Milenka. She prayed for the clank of Milenka's bell. Sometimes she thought she could hear it.

"Is that you, Milenka? Where are you?"

Her search took her all the way down past the duck pond and the elm tree, even to the old barn at the bottom of the farm.

A screech owl was crying. It was one of those sounds that belonged to the night, a lovely thrilling sound like the whinnying of a tiny horse. Where was Milenka? What had happened to her?

Now there were two screech owls tittering to each other. Their frail cries shivered under the stars. Tanya doubled back past the elm tree and the duck pond and took the lane up the hill, between the corn and wheat. Something scurried in the cornfield. She knew it couldn't be Milenka but she followed the sound into the stalks.

Whenever Tanya stopped, she heard the screech owls. She kept going, fighting her way uphill through the dead broken corn.

Then she saw Milenka, saw the silhouette of her sweet head and horns, and broke into a run. The cornstalks grabbed Tanya by the legs. She tore herself loose.

"You bad thing!" Tanya tried to sound angry, but she was laughing because she was so thankful. The corn slapped her in the face.

Milenka turned her head, revealing the Gypsy fire behind her.

CHAPTER
TWENTY-TWO

The fire burned hard and clean, the way timber burned only when it was dry; the Gypsies must have taken it from one of the woodpiles by the black pines. In the trembling shadows there were women with infants and men with knives in their belts. Horses grazed in the meadow. Someone whistled, and a horse ran in front of the white heart of the fire.

Tanya pulled on Milenka's collar, digging her heels into the ground. She slipped and hung from the collar, and stared through the cornstalks at the red and black shapes of the Gypsies.

Those screech owls she'd been hearing weren't screech owls at all, but Gypsy women, chanting some wordless song. They clapped their hands in time, and from somewhere came the beating of hands on the skins of little drums, like horses galloping. Then the moaning of a flute seemed to uncoil itself out of the darkness, and hovered and swayed like a cobra.

It wasn't music, it didn't sound like music, or like any music Tanya had ever heard. She hung from Milenka's collar with her knees to the ground. The Gypsy women clapped and shook as if in a trance. The men passed a bottle of spirits, and the women half-walked, half-danced to the gallop of the drums. A little girl drifted in front of the fire twirling her hands.

With a gasp, Tanya turned her face toward a rustling in the cornstalks. A young man and a girl stepped out of the corn together, their arms tight around each other's waists. In one hand the girl was carrying weeds and nettles.

As the lovers, moving as one, crossed the meadow toward the fire, Tanya's eyes followed them, and she saw the old woman standing behind the flames, the one motionless figure amid the pulsing of the dance. The firelight carved hollows in her face. Her hands were folded over her long gray braids. The lovers approached her, and the girl gave her the weeds and nettles. Tanya couldn't see everything because the black shapes of the dancers were wavering in front, but the old woman seemed to be looking closely at the plants. Some she threw into the fire. She finished her inspection, nodded to the girl and gave her what was left. The girl kissed her hand and hurried off, and Tanya remembered what Pavel had said about Gypsies and their poisons.

She saw the old woman lift her gaze from the fire. The shadows of her cheekbones made black wells of her eye sockets, but she seemed to be looking right where Tanya was, hanging from Milenka's collar. Something startled Tanya from behind. There was a flutter in the corn, and Vrana the crow flew past the fire's soaring sparks, to alight on the old woman's shoulder.

Tanya pulled herself to her feet. She saw the reflection of the fire in Milenka's round eye, and she cupped her hand over it so Milenka couldn't see. The eyelashes flicked against Tanya's palm, and she whispered into Milenka's ear.

"Milenka, listen to me!" Tanya felt the soft hairs against her mouth. "These people are bad. They'll hurt you. They don't love you. I love you. You belong to me. We're going home."

This time, Milenka yielded to the tug on her collar. Tanya held the tongue of the bell to keep it from ringing. She led Milenka downhill through the corn until she couldn't see the fire anymore. Then they cut across to the lane. The cries of the Gypsies rippled out over the hill. With every step Tanya felt a little safer. Every step brought them closer to the barn. But she kept looking up at the stars, because what frightened her most was the old woman's spy, that unnatural thing, a crow that could fly at night.

There were voices coming up the lane. Tanya couldn't see, but she heard the voices of two men.

When Milenka was in motion, nothing, least of all Tanya, could stop her; so at the sound of the voices Tanya did the first thing she thought of. She jumped up and hid behind Milenka. With one hand holding Milenka's collar, another hand at the scruff of her neck, and one leg up over the ribs, Tanya hung on.

The voices were those of two men. Tanya wasn't sure whom the first voice belonged to.

"Heaven protect us! It's the devil!"

The second voice was Pavel's.

"Calm down, will you? It's only the little girl's cow."

The two men dodged into the corn to get out of Milenka's way. They couldn't see Tanya hanging down the other side.

"That's it for me. When a cow makes me jump out of my skin, it's time to go home."

"Go home, you coward," Pavel said. "Go home to your fat wife and tell me about it in the morning. Don't you want to see the Gypsies? I can hear their music."

"Are you sure the women are beautiful?"

"Yes, I'm sure," Pavel said. "They're black as night and they've got hair like horses' tails."

It wasn't easy holding on to Milenka, and Tanya's feet touched down at the bottom of the lane. She hurried her cow to the barn, shut all the doors, and scooped her nightshirt and her parents' quilt off the ground.

All that night, she didn't light the lantern or even go

up to the hayloft. She stayed down below with Milenka in her stall, in case Vrana came to spy. But there was another reason to be with Milenka, and that was the measured sound of her breath, those puffs in the dark, to remind Tanya that some things in the world were still friendly, and gentle, and good. Tanya sat bunched up on the hay in a corner of the stall, with all her clothes on. For a long time she couldn't sleep.

Wrapped to her eyes in her parents' quilt, she saw the Gypsy fire coughing sparks at the stars; in the stillness of the barn, she heard the Gypsy music. It came from inside her like a heartbeat, and the women were clapping, shrieking, clinging to the heat of their fire, and she wished they would all catch on fire, burn up, and be ashes in the morning.

No, not even ashes: she wanted nothing to remain, not a trace, not a memory, nothing in the meadow and nothing in her mind. Tanya wanted her mind to go dark, as dark as a night without a fire, without a moon, without stars; without that awful clapping or those drums like a stampede of horses; without the voice of Pavel coming up the lane. What was Pavel doing there—Pavel, who hated Gypsies? What did he mean about the women having hair like horses' tails?

CHAPTER
TWENTY-THREE

She was lying on the grass and the sun was putting her to sleep, but her father kept chopping wood, and she wished he would stop. Every time she thought it was over, he did it again, and the wood split under the ax and tumbled with a clunky clatter, troubling her rest. It went on for too long, and the dream wore thin. Tanya woke up, and she knew it was Milenka coughing beside her in the stall.

"Milenka?" Tanya rose from the straw. Milenka's head was down. She seemed to be trying to push something out of her throat.

"Milenka, what did they do to you? Did they touch you? Did that old woman talk to you, or give you anything?"

Milenka coughed. Tanya reached up into her mouth and scraped her tongue. Her fingernails came out coated with white froth. She sniffed it. It smelled sour.

Tanya took the quilt from her shoulders and threw it over Milenka, then climbed to the hayloft to get the other quilts from the night before last. The little barn owls, the children, squeaked in their nest, and Tanya saw their three faces looking at her. She made sure the box with her money was still in its hiding place behind the oak timber, the tenth timber from the front of the barn. She counted them on her fingers, from her right thumb to her left thumb.

She draped Milenka in quilts to keep her warm, and went into the house to get the hearth going.

The day was summer-bright but winter-cold. Tanya built a fire in the hearth and filled a bucket at the well. Frost crackled underfoot, and the well water numbed her fingers. The water took time to warm over the fire. She carried the steaming bucket into the barn and sponged Milenka's forehead. She milked her, but the milk smelled bad, and she didn't want to take any chances with it. She emptied the pail into the ditch by the roadside.

Anton the Sharpener came up the road.

"Throwing away milk? Why, that's Nature's bounty, it is. Nature's bounty. Tut, tut."

Skinny Anton wasn't getting any fatter or any easier to look at. With his walking stick he looked like a wasp with a stinger, and with his grindstone he looked like one of those wasps that flew around in the summer carrying gobs of mud that weighed more than they did, to build their nests with, under the eaves of the barn.

"My Milenka's sick," Tanya said.

"Sick? Your dear cow is sick? Am I to presume, therefore, that today will be marked by the absence of muffins? By a skip, lacuna, or hiatus between the muffins of yesterday, and those of tomorrow?"

"I don't understand you when you talk like that."

"There's nothing to understand, except that muffins without milk are no muffins, but crackers, water biscuits, or at best, brittle cakes."

"There's some milk left over from yesterday, if you want a muffin," Tanya said.

"Please. But let us first examine this sick cow of yours."

Tanya walked him to the barn. "I didn't know you knew about animals, Anton," she said.

Anton wheeled about and swung his nose in her face. "Have you no *nose* for facts, child? Have you done nothing more in your short life than give short shrift to Anton? I know a thing or two or three. I know why cows are indisposed, why birds cheep, and what makes the roosters strut. I can read the heavens, and discuss the comings and goings of comets. I know why the sky blushes with shame when the night is over. I am more than a mere scientist of scissors." Anton screwed his walking stick into the ground. "I'm a philosopher," he said. "Apparently you've never met one before."

"What's a philosopher, Anton?"

"A lonely man, my little one; a lonely man."

Anton looked at Milenka in her stall. He looked her up and down and inside her ear. He pulled her eyelid back and looked at her startled eye staring back at him. He pinched her milk sack and tasted a drop of her milk. Then he stood back and pursed his lips.

"Well?" Tanya said.

"Gypsy fever," Anton said.

"Gypsy!" Tanya whispered.

Milenka coughed again.

"Gypsy fever. A disease caused by Gypsies."

Hearing Anton say it made it more real than Tanya could bear to believe. "She got out of the barn last night," Tanya said. "It was cold. Maybe she just caught a cold. Didn't you, Milenka?"

"Wasn't she near the Gypsies in your meadow?"

Anton knew everything. Tanya hugged Milenka's drooping head.

"What am I going to do, Anton?"

"You're going to make me a muffin, and listen to what I have to tell you."

CHAPTER
TWENTY-FOUR

Anton ate his muffin in the barn, because Tanya didn't want to be away from Milenka a minute more than she had to. She held Milenka's head in her arms and listened to Anton. He sat on the milking stool with the grindstone still on his back, and his voice sounded as though he were singing softly to himself.

"Before you were born, some Gypsies once camped along the river, up near the waterfalls. And there was a little girl in our village, who came home one day and told her parents she had made friends with some Gypsy children, and they had given her a delicious candy. She fell sick that very night.

"She turned pale and lost strength, and no one could do anything to cool her fever, and then the breath and pulse left the child, and her weeping parents laid her in the graveyard. Each day thereafter, the parents awoke with sinking hearts, for the first thing they thought of when they awoke was their dead child. The mother couldn't bear to visit the grave, but the father saw it each morning on the way out to his field, and his eyes always went to that little mound of fresh-turned earth.

"A week or so after the burial, on a misty morning, the father noticed the earth had been disturbed. He ran to the grave. It was dug up, the lumps of earth thrown to either side. The little coffin—he had made it himself from pine wood—was empty. Didn't your parents ever tell you this story?"

Tanya shook her head.

"I suppose they didn't want to frighten you. Well, all the villagers went out to the graveyard to see the empty grave, and they searched the fields and forests for miles around. They found nothing. The Gypsies had gone, of course; and the parents lost hope of ever knowing what had happened to the remains of their little girl.

"The days and weeks grew into months, and everyone still felt sorry for the parents, but not quite as sorry as in the beginning. Life goes on, you know. People forget. But not the parents, oh no! They lived alone with their grief. There were moments in the evenings when they would turn to one another and say that a wink, a heartbeat had passed in which they had failed to think of their daughter. And they would feel guilty for that moment of peace, and weep afresh in each other's arms.

"Then, almost a year later, a traveler came down from the mountains on his way to the sea. He passed through our village and stopped for a meal. Someone mentioned the little girl—how she got sick and died after the Gypsy children gave her candy. The traveler said that the very same thing had happened to a little boy in *his* village. But there the people had managed to catch a Gypsy, and had held him over a fire to make him talk, and what things he said!

"The Gypsy described a poison they have that heats you up with fever and puts you in a trance, a sleep that is deeper than sleep and seems in every way like death. Your family buries you, and the Gypsies sneak into the graveyard at night and dig you up out of the ground, and pour a broth down your throat, and you come back to life, but with no memory, no memory at all! You have forgotten the faces of your parents. You have forgotten your own house and your own name.

"Then the Gypsies who have poisoned you, they take you in their wagons through the maze of the pines, along secret trails, to the eastern lands of stony hills and hard sun, and farther still, to the great markets where camels and slaves are sold by the thousands. And there they sell you into slavery. And no one knows you, and no one will ever learn what has become of you.

"When the parents heard the traveler's report, their

lives were turned upside down all over again, and they did a thing that moved everyone to astonishment and pity. People in our village still talk about it. The parents sold their house, not for what it was worth but for a fraction of the true price, for they needed quick cash. They sold all their possessions, and set out to find their daughter.

" 'But where will you go?' people asked them. 'Where will you look?'

" 'We'll go to the East,' the parents said. 'We'll look wherever we can.' The villagers gathered on the bridge—you know which one—to watch the parents climb the road to the top of the hill. The villagers were praying and crossing themselves as if in the presence of some dreadful miracle of God, the love that would make a mother and father give up everything and search the world for their child, though they hardly knew where to look. Later we heard that at every village up the road, they asked everyone they met if they had seen Gypsies or a little girl. Later still, we heard that a shepherd saw two tiny figures, a man and a woman, trudging painfully across the snow fields in the mountains, heading eastward. And that was the last we ever heard of them."

The echo of Anton's voice died out in the hollows of the barn, and then, in the quiet, came the soft fluttering of the chickens in their coop. Once again, Milenka coughed. She dropped her head and coughed, and she seemed to be choking, and her ribs stood out when she coughed; and Tanya remembered the only thing that mattered to her now.

"But what about my Milenka?"

"Yes, I keep forgetting. You wouldn't have a dead horse lying around, would you?"

"A horse?"

"Yes, with the head still on, yes."

"I don't think so," Tanya said.

"Too bad. The skull would be useful. A horse's skull is very good against Gypsies. You stick it on a post where they can see it, and it scares them off."

"But Milenka's already sick."

"I know that. But if it scares the Gypsies, it just might weaken their spells. Your cow may start feeling better, and you can nurse her back to health. That's how magic works sometimes. It all makes quite a lot of sense, when you think about it."

"Help me, Anton!"

"I'll see what I can do." Anton got up from the milking stool. "Heavens, my legs are stiff. Getting old! I'm an old stub of a candle, I am. All burned down, I am. Nothing but a lot of waxy trickles and dribbles—one for each year of my life, I should think. Pretty soon they'll say, 'Enough! You've lived out your usefulness,' and they'll scrape me off the tabletop."

He took a last look at Milenka. "Keep her warm, keep her indoors, and keep the Gypsies out. I'll try to find you a horse's skull, and if all goes well, I'll be back with it first thing in the morning."

"Oh, thank you, Anton," Tanya said, wrapping her arms around Milenka's head.

"Don't mention it. I've enjoyed our conversation. It's so hard to find anyone who listens to old Anton and his tales."

As she opened the door for him, Tanya felt the force of the wind. Leaves and crows were flying, and the tree-tops shook. Anton hunched under his grindstone and clutched the lapels of his jacket close around his neck.

"Nippy," he said.

CHAPTER
TWENTY-FIVE

The geese and chickens were still outside, and Tanya moved quickly to feed them and get them in the barn. She fed them the way she always fed them, scraping corncobs with a knife and letting the kernels fall while the animals squawked and clucked and pecked. They would have liked more to eat, but she drove them into the barn early, the geese into their pen, the chickens into their coop. Two chickens wound up among the geese and one goose among the chickens. She grabbed the strays and dumped them in their proper places, shutting her eyes as their flapping shed feathers in all directions. The birds were on edge.

Tanya bolted the barn door. She was about to put the knife back in its place—on the shelf beside the lantern—but she stopped herself. She kept the knife.

She stabbed it into the wood of Milenka's stall where she could get it quickly in case the Gypsies came. She sat down on the hay in a corner, and gathered a quilt around her.

Milenka coughed. Tanya gave up her quilt and threw it over her cow.

"Is that better, Milenka?" Tanya settled down again in the corner of the stall. She didn't know what else to do but wait until morning for Anton to come back.

As she sat there, and the voices of the crows sailed back and forth over the barn, Tanya thought of her mother and father again. She didn't have to wonder where they were anymore, or what they were doing. They weren't doing anything. The river had washed them into the sea. There was no fisherman to find them, and no journey home. She would never see them, no matter how long she waited, no matter how long she lived.

They'd left her on the other side of the bridge with Milenka, to go on living without them. She should have stayed in the wagon with them. Why didn't she stay in the wagon?

She thought about that night. She remembered it from the beginning. The black raincloud that rolled over the village square and turned the day into night. The first raindrops smacking on the cobblestones, and everyone hurrying to close up. She remembered helping her parents load up the wagon with apples and pears and other things, and herself dropping an armful of apples and running to pick them up. She remembered the pounding of the rain, like fists, on the roof of the wagon. The roar in the river gorge. Her father snapping the reins to make the horse cross the bridge. The way the bridge shook when the tree slammed against it. The great branch of the tree sticking over the top of the bridge so that the wagon couldn't pass, and Milenka on the other side, standing out in the rain. And then her father, shouting at her.

"How many times have I told you to bolt that door?"

She jumped down from the wagon because he'd shouted at her.

His voice had sounded so angry. But he was right to be angry at her. She was supposed to have put Milenka in the barn and made sure to bolt the door. It wasn't the first time she hadn't done what she was supposed to do. She was always in a rush, or just not thinking, and she always failed to do that one thing, and it annoyed her father.

It was a little thing, but that didn't make it any less important. Her father used to say that every little thing you do makes a difference. When you build a woodpile, you don't just throw the pieces of wood on top of one another. You stack them carefully so they fit, because if you don't, the pile won't stand. Every piece of wood rests on the ones below it, the ones you lay first. What you do now will count later. Every good farmer lives by that rule, he used to say. And he would explain to her why he did this, why he did that, because a month from now, or a season from now, or years from now, it would make a difference. It's no good being careless or forgetful, even in the little things, because the little things add up.

Her father was right. Even an armful of apples added up—one-two-three-four-five, spilling from her arm to the cobblestones in the village square. If she hadn't dropped those apples, she wouldn't have had to chase after them as they rolled. She wouldn't have taken so much time when time was so precious, because every apple she dropped was a moment stolen from their safe return home. If she hadn't dropped those apples, they would have been on their way sooner. They would have gotten across the bridge before the tree barred the way, her mother and father would be alive now, and Gypsies wouldn't have poisoned Milenka.

Her father had shouted at her on the bridge, and it wasn't just the barn door he was talking about; it was the apples too, and the hundred times he'd told her not to be careless, the hundred lessons he'd tried to teach her. Time and again he'd told her this, told her that, because he loved her, because he cared about her;

and she never listened. Why didn't she ever listen to her father? If she'd loved him more, she would have listened to him.

"*Now* do you see what I mean?" she heard him saying in his anger. "*Now* look what you've done!"

CHAPTER
TWENTY-SIX

The barn door rattled. Someone was trying to get inside the barn.

Tanya shut the gate of the stall and went to the door. But she didn't open it.

"Who's there?"

No one answered. Sometimes the wind could take the barn door and shake its panels and make it sound as though someone were there. Tanya could hear the wind outside, feel it forcing its way under the door.

Then her stomach spoke up. She was hungry. There was food in the house, the heel of a loaf of bread, and she should go get it now, before the sun went down. Already the light coming in under the door was a sunset light, pale and pinched with cold.

The wind bumped against the door.

"Milenka, I'll be right back," Tanya said, lifting the

plank that bolted the handles together. She swung the panels open—and those three little Gypsies, the boy and two girls who'd taunted Pavel yesterday, flew inside the barn.

"Get out! Go away!" she shouted at them. The children screamed and squealed and ran up and down the length of the barn. Tanya stood in front of Milenka's stall with her arms thrown back against the gate.

"Leave us alone! Go away!"

The girls ran with their long black hair streaming. The boy pulled the pitchfork off the wall and danced with it like a devil. The girls clapped to his dance, and Tanya kept shouting.

"Go away!"

The boy jabbed the pitchfork at Tanya. She clamped her eyes shut and felt the rusty points about to go into her stomach, and she heard herself shouting the same thing over and over.

That was all she heard. She opened her eyes to see the points of the pitchfork swinging in front of her, but the girls had it now, their eyes and teeth flashing under the hair spilling over their faces. The smaller girl was jumping up and down next to her sister, squeaking and jabbering in Gypsy.

Now the boy was in the chicken coop, driving the birds wild. He crawled out with one poor frightened creature flapping in his dirty hands. He squeezed and twisted its neck. The chicken's eyes bugged out, and then the Gypsy boy tore its head off.

You couldn't grow up on a farm without seeing that sort of thing many times. Tanya had seen it, and she would always shut her eyes or look away and feel sorry for the chickens. But she'd never seen anyone do it with such glee. The blood came out in gobs—glug glug glug—and then began to spray, and the boy held the chicken like a hose and sprayed Tanya.

When she took her hands from her face, she was alone.

"Milenka. Are you all right?" Tanya wiped the blood from her eye.

But the Gypsies hadn't touched Milenka.

Click clack.

It came from the barnyard. Click clack.

It was little Nikola with his blocks, sitting on his knees in front of the house, a dim little shape in the shadows of the dying day. The sun was taking one last look at the land, and the sky behind the thatch burned a fierce pink.

"Go home, Nikola! No muffins! No muffins today! Go home!"

Though the barn door was wide open, Nikola couldn't hear her, and it wouldn't have made any difference if he could. Tanya knew she'd have to go out and push him on his way. She turned to Milenka:

"Don't worry, Milenka. I won't leave you." She ran out.

Even as she ran to him, Nikola didn't look up, but played and thought of nothing, like a lamb in a country of wolves.

"Nikola, go home! It's not safe here. Gypsies, Nikola! Gypsies! Go home!"

She took him by the arm and brought him out to the road. She didn't see any Gypsies. But they could be hiding anywhere.

"Go on home, Nikola! Go!"

She pushed him to get him started down the hill. But he turned and looked at her, looked right into her eyes, as if he didn't want to go; and Tanya knew why Mother Anna loved him so much, with his round eyes under his little cap and his cheeks rosy from the cold.

"No, Nikola. You can't stay here. Go home, go home!"

Should she go with him, or at least take him across the bridge? But what if the villagers saw her with him? They would never understand.

Someone—she couldn't see who it was—was fishing on the bridge, staring down at his line as though studying his face in a mirror. He lifted his head.

"Go home, Nikola," Tanya said softly, like a prayer. She watched as Nikola walked away. He was going down the road, back to the village. She heard crows in the sky and hurried back to the barn.

It got dark in there fast. The owl children awoke in the hayloft. The geese and chickens were silent. Even Milenka seemed to be sleeping. At least she wasn't coughing anymore. Tanya didn't light the lantern. She sat in Milenka's stall, leaning against the wood. She was still hungry. She felt frail and empty.

Ghosts must feel this way, she thought. Now she knew how they could walk through walls. She lay down on the straw and kept going, down into the world of the ghosts.

She slept for hours. It was almost midnight when a loud noise awakened her. Gypsies. The Gypsies were outside. They were trying to break into the barn. They were ramming the door.

In the dark Tanya groped for her knife. It was stuck somewhere in the wood of the stall. She caught a splinter in her hand. There wasn't time to pull it out. She found the knife. The barn door began to give way, and she held the knife with both hands, ready to cut the first Gypsy that came near.

CHAPTER
TWENTY-SEVEN

The door burst open with a blaze of torches—more than Tanya could count—torches in the hands of people she couldn't see, because the gate of the stall was taller than she, and she was crouching all the way in the back.

"Blood! There's blood over here!"

"Oh my God."

A woman screamed.

"Oh no!"

"Look everywhere! Look up there!" Footsteps pounded on the planks of the hayloft. Bits of old hay came drizzling down from the cracks. Tanya squeezed into the corner of the stall and held the knife out in front of her. The Gypsies were going to find her any second.

"Nothing up here."

"Are you sure?"

"Something over here!"

"Where?"

"It's just an owl's nest."

Just as Tanya started to wonder how she could understand Gypsy, she realized they weren't Gypsies at all. They were the villagers.

They swung open the gate of the stall. Torches and lanterns poked in.

"She's here!"

"Watch out for the cow! Keep clear of the horns."

"Careful! She's got a knife."

"There's blood on her."

"She's covered with blood!"

The torches were too bright. She heard the whoosh of the flame as someone swung a torch. It hit her hand and the knife fell to the ground.

"Grab her!"

"Keep the torch on the cow! Get that gate shut!"

Tanya fought and kicked.

"Grab the leg!"

They half-dragged, half-carried her out to the barnyard. One of them thrust his hard strained face at her. It was Pavel.

"How did you get the blood on you?"

Pavel pulled and twisted her sweater at the shoulders. The stitches were bursting.

"Whose blood is this? Tell me!"

She tried to tell him.

"What? What are you saying?"

"Chicken—Gypsies—"

"What about the Gypsies?"

"They were here!" Tanya said. "They killed a chicken."

She could see him thinking, trying to figure out if she was telling the truth. As his eyes searched hers, she caught the voices around her.

"She says they killed a chicken."

"I don't believe her."

"She's lying!"

They pressed around her. She saw the blade of a sickle and the twin barrels of a shotgun hanging down. Everyone's breath steamed in the cold, and the wisps went up like smoke from chimneys among the torches.

Pavel shook her. "Where is he? Where's my son?"

Nikola must have vanished on the way home. Pavel spoke Tanya's next thought for her:

"You were seen with our little Nikola! You were the last one with him!"

The villagers were going through the house too. Something big came out and parted the crowd. The hands lifted Tanya into the air like a pair of horns, and behind the horns was Mother Anna's face, the face of a mad blue-eyed bull.

"What have you done to my baby?"

Mother Anna's face started going up and down. The

torches went up and down and blurred. Mother Anna was shaking Tanya, shaking her, shaking her.

"What have you done to my baby?"

Tanya's head went back and forth so hard, her teeth banged together. Mother Anna was screaming at her. The shaking wouldn't stop.

"I saw—I saw them!" Tanya said.

"You saw what? What? What did you see?" came many voices at once.

The shaking stopped; and to keep it from starting again, Tanya said: "I saw them take Nikola."

The women cried out. Mother Anna flung Tanya aside—the torches streaked like shooting stars. Tanya landed on some man's muddy shoes and the cold dirt of the barnyard. She was surrounded by legs, and the legs were all going in the same direction, and the men were shouting above her.

"Blood of an innocent!"

"Load your guns."

Someone barked in Tanya's ear:

"Where do you think you're going?"

The hand that grabbed her wrist was big and round and rugged with callouses, as she remembered her father's hand. But this hand wasn't gentle. The villagers charged around the barn, past the well and up the orchard, and the hand made her go with them. Tanya had to run just to keep from falling. The lanterns and the blowing flames of the torches sent shadows up and down and around, and the blades of the scythes and points of the pitchforks banged against the branches and chopped twigs off the apple trees. Some of the villagers tripped in the holes in the ground.

"Watch it with that blade, you almost killed me!"

"What the hell are these holes?"

"It's the Gypsies. They were here, digging for gold."

"Thieves!"

There were villagers in front of her, behind her and on either side, running, stumbling, still running, like children chased by bees. Behind Tanya were the old people, the grandmothers and grandfathers, moving as fast as their old legs could carry them, as though they had waited all their lives for this moment. The old ones were saying:

"We'll burn the Gypsies. We'll burn them tonight."

"They'll pay. I swear to God, they'll pay."

"A throat for every drop of that little boy's blood."

"We'll slit their kids' throats and make their mothers watch."

"We'll cut their kids' eyes out with rusty spoons."

A hole in the orchard swallowed her captor's foot. He spilled forward and hit the ground in a squish of rotten apples. Tanya turned and ran.

It didn't matter where she put her feet. She seemed to fly down the orchard, barely touching the ground. Let them trip and fall and huff and puff—they could never catch her now. She ran past an old man hobbling on a cane and an old couple helping each other along. The cold air jumped down her throat. Tanya had her brief escape, her little share of freedom, and then she smelled hay burning.

A shadow came out the owl door on the side of the barn. It looked like a puff of smoke at first. It was the barn owl, faster than smoke, flying up with a feathery bundle in her talons. Tanya ran so hard, she couldn't feel her legs anymore, just the ground banging on the soles of her feet. And yet she felt almost calm inside. She knew what she was doing. Her mind was clear. There was a fire in the hayloft. The hay must have caught fire from the villagers' torches. Milenka was still in her stall.

Think, Tanya told herself—don't be careless again. Grab a bucket from the well and try to put the fire out.

Up from the bottom of the well came the sound of the bucket hitting the water. Tanya looked back at the barn. She couldn't see inside it. Creamy smoke, the smoke of hay, oozed from the thatch. She freed the brimming bucket from the rope.

Not until she lugged the bucket in front of the door did she feel the heat or hear the birds screeching or Milenka crashing against the gate of her stall. Tanya let go of the bucket to open the chicken coop and the geese pen. She flicked the latch to Milenka's gate. Milenka burst out of her stall and almost trampled her.

Milenka still had the quilts on, and the quilts had

caught fire. Tanya ripped them away, picked up the bucket, and swung it with a strength she didn't know she had. Drops of water splashed in her face, and Milenka, wild-eyed, turned this way and that in the middle of the barn, bewildered by the flames.

"Go outside, Milenka! Run!" Tanya said, and gave her a push.

In the burning barn she pushed Milenka once. A strange feeling came over her. She didn't know what it was. She felt her hands going to Milenka again as though the hands would have an answer for her. So she pushed again, and it was on that second push that she journeyed through time.

She was taken back to that night on the bridge with her parents. She didn't remember it, she relived it—all because Milenka's hide was wet from the splash of the bucket. Her hide felt just as it did that night when Tanya ran across the bridge and pushed her toward the barn. The same hide, the same hands, the same Tanya.

She was taken back. Milenka's hide seemed as thin as paper, Tanya's hands went through it, and her whole body shot forward. She left the barn behind her—it was like dashing on a horse through a fiery tunnel and out the other side. The sound of the flames twanged like a string and deepened to the roar of the river, the water in her eyes became the rain, and she was back on the bridge with her parents.

They were riding in the wagon and the tree slammed

against the bridge, and the bridge shook, and her father shouted at her.

"How many times have I told you to bolt that door? Run and put Milenka inside! Run!"

She could feel the edge of his voice cutting into her, and she jumped down from the wagon. "Be careful, Tanya," she heard her mother say. But her father's voice mattered more, and then came the icy water biting at her feet, soaking her shoes as she splashed through it. She ducked under the branch of the tree that held the bridge in its grasp.

Now that it was happening again, Tanya understood it better. The water at her feet wasn't the rain—it was too cold. It was the river. The tree had cracked the bridge open, and her father knew it. He knew that the river was about to break the bridge in two, and that there wasn't time for all three of them to get down from the wagon and save themselves.

"Run!"

She ran across the bridge and put her hands on Milenka.

"Run, Milenka!" Tanya said, and as she lifted her hands she was flung back through the fiery tunnel, and the barn was burning around her.

Milenka went bounding out the door. Tanya followed her, fighting through a blizzard of geese and chickens. The birds fluttered and fell, and loose feathers were flying. And out under the stars, with the barn at her back, Tanya gulped the sweet air into her lungs and sobbed for her parents.

Her father wasn't angry at her on the bridge. He just sounded that way, to make her run without asking why or looking back. She didn't look back. She didn't see her father's face or her mother's face or see them take each other's hand as they sent her on her way. "Be careful, Tanya," her mother had said; and they let her go.

It seemed so long ago, a lifetime ago; so much had happened since. She'd been through so much. If only she could have her parents back for just a moment, she could tell them she understood.

But if they came back even for a moment, they would see what was happening to the barn.

Her money. The box with her money was still in there.

What made her remember it now? She didn't know. That box was all she had. That was why she'd hidden it so well. It was up in the hayloft where no one would find it, behind an oak timber—the tenth timber from the front of the barn.

Maybe the fire hadn't gotten to it yet. Maybe it wasn't too late. She ran back in.

The smoke blinded her. She found the ladder by running smack into it. Her hands and feet pulled and pushed her up the ladder's rungs. She was almost to the hayloft when the fire blew a hole in the roof.

Not once, in all the times Tanya had lit the oven and listened to the air rumbling through the vent, did she ever think she would one day be inside a place like that. Now she was. From the door the wind went rushing up through the hole in the roof, and blew Tanya's skirt inside out like a broken umbrella.

But at least the wind blew the smoke out with it, and Tanya could see, she could breathe. She crawled onto the planks of the hayloft. The wind whistled through the cracks.

Clumps of hay rolled over her into the fire. The fire was inhaling them. She was afraid to look, but she had to. She had to open her eyes and count the timbers. She counted on her fingers—one two three four five, nearer the flames—her hair blew in her face and she lost count. She started over—one two three four five six seven eight—she stopped. The tenth timber was in the fire.

A minute earlier, maybe when she was saving Milenka, Tanya could have thrown the hay aside and taken the box out with her bare hands. She couldn't get it now without something to reach with.

The pitchfork. Where was it? She hadn't seen it since the Gypsy children had it.

She threw her leg over the ladder, climbed back down and looked for the pitchfork. A chicken swept past her in the updraft. The pitchfork was hanging in its usual place on the front wall. One of the villagers must have picked it up and put it there. It would be just like them to do that. Never leave pitchforks lying around. Somebody could get hurt.

The ladder went on and on, rung after rung. At last Tanya got the pitchfork and herself over the edge of the hayloft. She got close to the fire, hiding her face under her arm, trying to work the pitchfork behind the timber and pull the box loose. Her hair crackled around her ears, and she could feel the skin on her arm curdling like milk.

From behind the timber, the box tumbled out, smoking. She dragged it toward her, then took the hem of her skirt and the box in her hand, using her skirt like a kitchen cloth when she took the hot muffin pan from the oven. She held the box bundled in her skirt and started down the ladder. Her free hand darted from one rung to the next.

Her foot slipped, and she fell.

CHAPTER
TWENTY-EIGHT

She fell, and then she wasn't falling anymore but floating upward on the smoke. The hayloft broke apart and the planks twirled in the air and she rose through the hole in the roof. The smoke made her cough. It was laced with sparks. She saw the house and the barn and the high meadow with the villagers' torches twinkling like fireflies on a summer evening. The smoke lifted her over the river gorge and the bridge and the red tiles of the village rooftops.

What puzzled her was the sunset, because she was sure the sun had gone down hours ago. It was setting now. It cast a glorious light over the land and winked goodbye. The barn burned in the dark of the night, and she thought: Barns make the best fires.

When the smoke blew against her back, she saw the

stars. They were closer, not tiny points as they seemed from the earth, but beads of polished silver. The higher she went, the thicker the smoke, and it was still choking her. Just when she thought she couldn't stand it anymore, she was among clouds, pink and golden towering clouds, grand as thunderheads, gentle as doves.

She thought it was more beautiful than anything she had ever seen in her life; and as soon as she thought it, she knew it was true. She had died in the barn, and these were the clouds of heaven. Suddenly she was so happy. Even amid the flames of the barn, she couldn't forget the lie she'd told about the Gypsies—about seeing them take Nikola—and she couldn't forget what the villagers had said after that. It was terrible, what words could do, what words could mean. She didn't mean what she said about the Gypsies. She said it because she was frightened. Now that she saw the clouds and how beautiful they were, she thought that God had understood, and had forgiven her.

Clouds upon clouds, like fantastic castles in the embers of a fire; and inside the clouds were birdlike things, flocks of them flying up. They must be angels, the souls of children, of others like herself, who had died young and were still new to heaven. She would join them in a moment—no, if this was heaven, her parents were here, and she would join them. Her heart beat fast, and an angel came, flapping its wings to her heartbeats.

No words had to be spoken. She understood it all.

The angel had come to take her to her parents. It welcomed her with wings thrown back like arms about to embrace her. It clapped its wings for her, the way her parents clapped on her birthday. Today was her birthday, her first day in heaven, and her parents were near. She could feel them. The angel's wings were wings of flame. The feathers were burning. The feathers were falling off. The angel was burning. The angel was dying. It was a goose on fire, shaking the ashes of its feathers into Tanya's mouth.

There was no heaven, no angel. Tanya was lying on the floor of the barn. She screamed and rolled over on her stomach, away from that horrible flapping burning thing. She felt her box under her, the box and its loose lid. She took them and ran.

She ran out into the night—not far, just to the bottom of the field—she felt so weak that when she dropped her box and its lid, she sank to her knees on the cold grass and the hot tatters of her skirt.

Just three coins slid from side to side in her charred box. She pawed the grass around her, searching for the others. She crawled on her hands and knees, sweeping and raking the grass with her fingers. Her fingers found pieces of twigs and leaves and a cold marble from the old days, and for a moment she thought it was what she wanted because it was round and seemed precious. She held it to the light of the barn and saw the glint in the eye of the marble, and threw it from her. She kept searching, but every new turn forced her to face the truth that her money was back in the fire, lost when she fell from the ladder.

Three coins, three pence were left—that, and the blackened roses and stars on the box, the gift, once, of Mother Anna.

The roof of the barn caved in, groaning and thundering, but the noise was faint to Tanya. Sitting on her knees with her box in her hands, she stopped thinking, stopped remembering, stopped worrying, stopped hoping. Her mind went dark. The fog that had come once before—the fog that had possessed her the morning after her parents died, the morning the villagers found her in the house and Mother Anna put her in the copper basin and bathed her—the fog came over her again. It wrapped itself around her like a sea fog around a lighthouse, dimming its light. Nothing mattered anymore, nothing seemed real, nothing but the ache that slowly settled under her and took shape in her legs. She had been sitting on her legs for too long. She got up and started walking, drifting.

Her old swing came softly toward her, like a ghost sliding her a chair. Tanya had wandered under the elm. She sat on the swing. It wobbled backward. She put the box down and touched the ropes.

Something glittered in front of her. It was long and thin and lay on its side, a ribbon of yellow stars, very bright and clear. It held her eyes. Tanya pushed the ground away from her with her feet. Each time she pushed, the swing tried to return, and she began to sway on the long ropes that hung from the branch of the elm.

It took that shifting, that swaying, for the yellow stars to come into focus, to find a place in the darkness. It was the duck pond. The elm had shed its leaves on the black mirror of the water, and the barn burned there, upside down. That was what glittered among the fallen leaves on the water.

Tanya lifted her eyes, and the barn, right side up, smoldered inside its stone walls. The house too was on fire, a fresh fire on the roof. Sparks must have blown over from the barn and kindled the thatch. The house wore its new flames like a crown.

Legs straight out as she swung forward. Legs bent as she swung back. Tanya pumped on her swing. Toes to the sky. Calves to the wood. She cut through the air. Her stomach swooped down after her, and the ropes creaked on the branch. Tanya swung in long deep arcs of forgetfulness, under the unbending strength of the elm. She threw her head back. Her hands held tight. Her legs were wings taking her away, while her house burned down.

She belonged to the air, until the air got colder. Her arm was hurting, burning. She had to stop. Her feet bumped on the bare patch of earth under the swing. She cradled her arm. Her sleeve was all but torn off.

Pavel had done that when he shook her and twisted her sweater. The wool had a big hole in it. She was shivering from the cold.

Taking her box, she started walking again. She was still in her fog, but somewhere in the back of her mind she must have been looking for shelter, because she wound up by the old barn at the bottom of the farm.

She'd been there before, once or twice in her life. Under the old barn's broken roof were rusty plows and harrows tangled up in vines. The doors were gone, the rafters sagged. Every farm, no matter how pretty, had a place like the old barn, where things of the past were left to the vines, to get tangled up and rot like flies in cobwebs.

The grass grew high around the walls. Tanya stepped into one of the old wagon ruts in the forgotten road into the woods. Burrs caught her skirt. The grass rustled. The rustling grew large in front of her, and she knew it was the echo in the belly of the old barn, with its door open to receive her.

There was a smell of dead animal and mold. She didn't mind the smell so much. Her arm bothered her more, and she needed to lie down. She met a stone wall and slumped against it.

Sleep came at once, but not to stay. It was a nervous sleep, flitting like a moth around a flame, and her arm was the flame.

Click clack.

Tanya saw the moth's face, gloomy and brown, and then she was wide-awake.

Clack.

The sound was coming from behind her, from the other side of the stone wall. In the old barn the stalls were divided by stone.

Click.

With her hands to guide her, Tanya crept toward the sound. She felt along the wall, felt the smooth granite stones and the patches of flaking mortar. She felt the wall's end, and looked around into the dark of the other side.

Click.

A match was scratched against the wall, and the green flash fell on little Nikola. Tanya saw the long fingers of the man holding the match, the greasy hair stuck to his pale forehead, and his eye; and at first she didn't recognize him without his grindstone.

CHAPTER
TWENTY-NINE

The little stall had once been a sheepfold, and a fuzz of wool hairs lay on the floor. The rafters were so low that if Anton stood up he'd hit his head. From one rafter hung a string, its other end tied around Nikola's waist to keep him from running away. Nikola sat happily playing with his blocks. He had his coat buttoned up and his cap on, just as Tanya had last seen him, when she'd sent him down the road to go home.

"Good heavens!" Anton said. "What on earth happened to your hair? It's all frizzled to bits. Little girls with pretty hair should stay out of burning barns. You look like hell itself, you've got an ash moustache, and you smell like the devil's own fart. And blood—whose blood is that? You wouldn't have blood on your conscience, now would you, Muffin Child?"

Even the finger of flame wagging on Anton's match frightened Tanya, and she threw her arm over her face. But still she noticed, beneath the arm and her torn sleeve, the checkered cloth on the ground in front of Anton. On the cloth were a half-eaten loaf of bread, a sausage, a pocket knife, and a brown jug. Tanya lowered her arm, and Anton saw her looking at the food.

"Would you like some sausage?" Anton said, and the match went out. He spoke in the dark.

"My mother's sausage. I don't think you've ever met my mother. Pleasant old soul. Cheerful. Doesn't get around much. And do you know what she says? Never slice a sausage too thick. Kills the taste."

Another match flared, and now Anton was pointing his knife at Tanya, with a thin slice of sausage stuck on the end. He passed the match behind the slice, and it glowed like a paper lantern.

"See how the light leaks through it. That's the test. Go ahead, take it. Don't be shy."

Tanya knelt down and took it.

"Tasty, yes. Tastes so good it hurts, doesn't it? Sometimes it's best to go hungry for a while, just to be able to taste food again."

He cut her a piece of bread. After the first couple of mouthfuls, her stomach stopped crying at her, and her eyes went to Nikola.

"He's fine," Anton said, and tugged at the brim of Nikola's cap.

Nikola was rolling his blocks like wheels.

"Yes, little man, amuse yourself," Anton said. "Play with those blocks of yours. Play, play. That's the spirit. The world in a grain of sand. Not a hard one to please, are you? Up past your bedtime, aren't you the lucky one! What an adventure! What a lark! A few hours more, and you'll be on your way. The sun will be near rising and the land will be blue, with a silver frost. The cold will make your eyes water, and you'll see the Morning Star weeping. There'll be a farmer out walking, yes, with a night's beard on his face, and he'll take you by the hand and cry out the news in the village streets, and the shutters will open, and the shouts of joy will be heard over the rooftops, and there'll be happiness, such happiness! All the village will rejoice, and the day will dawn, a day without Gypsies."

The dark swallowed Anton's match. He lit another, and as he went on talking, he lit matches, one after the other. His voice kept going in the matchlight and the dark, that soft dreamy voice that seemed to lull you half to sleep.

"Come, come now, Muffin Child. Don't make such a face. When I was a little boy—just about the age of our friend here—a man in our village cut his finger on a saw. He washed the finger well, tied it with a bandage, and did his best to forget about it. But it throbbed and throbbed, and when he took the bandage off, the whole finger was green and full of pus, and stank to high heaven.

"There was only one thing to do. I was there when they did it. The poor fellow. Thwack! Down came the hatchet, and the green finger lay all by itself in a puddle of blood. Such hollering there was! But the next time I saw him, the hand had healed, and he was back at work, nine-fingered, pink-cheeked and cheerful.

"You see, if they hadn't chopped that finger off, the sickness and the pus would have taken the hand, and then the arm, and then the whole of him. Something had to be done. Not an easy thing, not a pleasant thing, and not for the faint of heart. But it had to be done. Do you get my point yet?

"In a few hours our little friend here will come bumbling out of the shadows of the darkest night in our village in many a year. The dew will kiss his face, and his mother will kiss his face, and it will be as though this night never was. The memory of it will hang over them. Each one will know what the other is thinking, and the knowledge will leap from eye to eye like lightning over the hills, but the eyes will turn away, and the rain will never come.

"They'll talk about it all right—but later, much later. They won't be able to bear the silence anymore, and talking will make them feel better. They'll talk in little groups, all the while looking over their shoulders to be sure that no one else hears. And do you know what they'll say?

" 'I'm not proud of what I did,' one will say to the other. 'I'm not either,' the other will say. 'When we went up to the Gypsies looking for the little boy, and we saw those bones boiling in that Gypsy soup pot, we should have known they were the bones of the sheep they'd stolen. Yes, we should have known. A sheep's bones don't look anything like the bones of a little boy—no, not in the light of day, when everyone's calm, and you have time to think! But it was dark up there, we were running around crazy and frightened, things were happening so fast, and the truth is that we wanted to find that little boy dead. Yes, we wanted to find his bones. We wanted to get our hands on the thing that was torturing us in our minds, just to end the torture. We never found his head, did we? Of course not! We were so sure the Gypsies had it! Remember what we did to that old woman to make her tell? Never mind, let's not talk about it. Why torture ourselves all over again? Our only witnesses were the stars.

" 'What's done is done,' they'll say. 'We did what we thought was right at the time. We were wrong, but we were right. We had to protect our children.' Oh, the things people will do in the name of protecting their children."

Anton crooked his finger through the handle of his jug and tipped it to his mouth. He drank, and said:

"Pardon me. Where are my manners? Here, you must be thirsty."

He handed the jug to Tanya.

She took a swallow. It was brandy. She started coughing.

Anton turned his head to the side. He'd heard a sound. Tanya heard it, and she held her breath to listen. It sounded like someone else was coughing too. It came from the high meadow—shotguns going off, blast after blast—a heavy muffled sound, like a man coughing into his hand.

A smile crossed Anton's lips. He lifted his hand and touched one fingertip to another. "They're chopping the finger off. To save the hand. To save the arm. To save us all."

Tanya heard screams.

"You think I'm a bad man, don't you?" Anton said. "But why? I'm not up there shooting Gypsies. The good people of our village are!"

He took another drink. The liquor swished inside the jug.

"They came to *you* first. I saw them. I was sitting on your little swing. I saw everything. What did you tell them, Muffin Child? What did you say, to send them running for the Gypsies?

"But I wouldn't worry much if I were you. You'll learn to live with your conscience. We all do, in the end. It's what makes the world go round."

The last match had gone out, and Anton grunted as he got up.

"Old age! It's the final insult. You'll excuse me for a moment, won't you?"

He steadied himself on Tanya's shoulder. The touch of his hand came and went, and his footsteps trudged away in the dark. She heard him yawning, then nothing, and then she heard him pee.

She looked up at the hole in the roof, and saw the stars.

Anton was coming back, dragging his feet like a tired old man. Tanya was tired too, and still hungry. She leaned forward to take another piece of bread. It was a hard-crusted loaf. She felt around for the knife. She felt the cloth. The sausage. The jug. No knife.

If she hadn't been leaning forward, the knife would have gotten her. Anton just missed her. The steel scraped the stone wall and made a spark, a little green light like the flicker under the bedsheet at night when you lift it up and scratch it with your feet.

Now began a mad dance under that patch of starlight through the roof, with Anton jabbing and slashing and Tanya dodging him, covering her face with her box. The three coins flew around inside.

"I can't trust you not to tell," Anton said.

She couldn't see him. He couldn't see her.

"Hold still. Hold still and let me kill you quickly."

His invisible arm swooped and hummed through the air.

"Don't force me to wound you first. Give yourself up, and it will be over in a second! You won't even feel my blade! This is the Sharpener talking to you!"

Time and again, Tanya had watched Anton sharpen things. It was always a wonder to see. He would take his grindstone off his back and set it gently on the ground, pump the pedal and make the blade sing, sing, sing. Anton loved his work. He would smile with closed lips and rock the blade like a baby, lending it a fine bright edge that twinkled with menace . . .

Anton slipped around behind her, and she felt his breath on her neck. Her life was over.

But it wasn't. It wasn't Anton. Behind Tanya was a horse, crunching a bit in its mouth. On the horse sat a man. He had entered the place just now, all but silently in the dark. He and Anton faced each other, as though each knew who the other was. The rider slid down, and by the slippery sound Tanya could tell he'd been riding bareback. He glided past her with a sweet scent of oil in his hair, and spoke to Anton with a chuckle in his voice and an accent she couldn't place:

"So you are good with a knife, my friend? I wish to see how good you are."

Tanya bolted. She ran from the barn, leaving the two men facing each other in the shadows. She ran and kept running. Her burning house lit up the night. She heard galloping. A blast of thunder and horse knocked her down as a Gypsy stormed by, right in front of her. She got up, staggered and turned.

Two more riders galloped past, so close that a speck of foam, warm at first and then cold, smacked her cheek. She couldn't go forward, couldn't go back. She was caught in the middle of them.

From the orchard, from the field the riders came, shouting to each other in Gypsy. There was a man with a head wound, wiping and blinking the blood from his eyes. There were two boys together on a pony. There was a girl with a long braid in the wind, riding like she was born on a horse, and she turned her head and looked at Tanya.

Another horse leapt out of the corn and the rider tipped sideways. Tanya didn't move, but stared at the rider, thinking he was wounded and was going to fall off his horse. He was leaning down and his long arm was hanging. The arm reached out and took her breath away. He had her by the waist. Her feet were off the ground. The muscles in the horse's shoulder were beating against her, and she gazed at the Gypsy's moustache that went all the way back to his ear.

The Gypsy wagons were rumbling down the hill to meet the riders at the bottom of the farm. Now there were teams of horses together and wagon wheels bumping on the grass. The arm that held Tanya lifted her and threw her away. She went flying through space.

They say that if you lie out under the stars all night, you can see the whole sky turn like a wheel around the North Star. Tanya saw something like that in an instant of time when the rider threw her to another Gypsy in the front seat of a wagon.

Strong hands received her and passed her back through a little door. The wagon was bouncing, and it was filled with the smells of old blankets and spices that tickled the inside of her nose. Two children were sobbing in the arms of an old woman with long gray braids.

A pair of black wings came in through the little door with an ear-splitting caw. Vrana the crow clutched the old woman's shoulder and cawed with fright and anger, the way crows cry out when farmers shoot at them. Tanya saw the pointed little tongue, and her ears seemed to hear words trapped inside the harsh notes.

"She's the one! She's the one! She lied about us!"

Branches banged against the wagon. The Gypsies were fleeing down the old forgotten road into the woods.

CHAPTER
THIRTY

No one laid a hand on Tanya. No one spoke to her. Vrana hushed, and the Gypsy children cried themselves to sleep. From under the wagon came the slow rumbling of the wheels. Tanya heard the groans of the wounded, and owls calling across the night.

Twice the banging of the branches stopped, telling her that the wagons were out in the open, in a field or a clearing. But always they went back into the womb of the woods. The sounds of the branches changed. Needles swiped softly against the wagon, and Tanya knew that the Gypsies had entered a pine forest.

They left her alone inside the wagon. She heard the chink of shovels, and she lifted the rags at the window to see people digging in the gleam of lanterns behind the trees. The Gypsies were burying their dead. Tanya couldn't look—she got down on the floor and put her knees to her chin. The Gypsies began to wail. The moment had come to give the departed to the earth. The screams rose to such a pitch, Tanya thought the villagers had followed the Gypsies and were attacking again. She couldn't bear the screams. She put her hands over her ears, but that couldn't stop the voice inside her that said it was all her fault, people had died because of her.

As the graves were closed—the dirt was shoved back, and tamped with the flat of the shovels—the Gypsies seemed to cough and laugh, but it was only their exhausted grief.

The hands over Tanya's ears curled into fists and pounded on her head, pounded, pounded; and there was a crackling around her ears, the crackling of ashes, of her hair shorn by the fire and burned to ashes. It didn't feel like her own hair anymore. It felt like Milenka, the hard short hairs, the feel of Milenka under the palm of her hand.

That was when Tanya stopped thinking about herself, how bad she was and how bad she felt; and she remembered Milenka. Milenka was alone on the farm, burned by the fire, lost without her, waiting for her to come back. Milenka needed her. Tanya didn't know what she would do when she found her, or where they would go. She had to get back to the farm, and take care of her.

Her parents had never come back, but she would; she would find her way back to the one living thing she still had the power to help. She hopped down from the wagon. The road was at her feet. A gust of wind went howling through the pines.

The road was overgrown and the old ruts were hard to see because there was no moon. But like a bird navigating by the stars, Tanya let herself be guided by the starlight between the two black walls of the pines.

This kept her on the road, except where it crossed open land; and just as Tanya had guessed from inside the wagon, there were two open places. She lost the ruts first in a meadow, and she had to search the meadow's edge for the gap in the pines, where the road kept going.

Further on, she came to the other clearing. Part of it was someone's old potato field. In the softening light she could see the square shapes of woodpiles standing like houses. Deer were grazing. The buck stamped his hoof at her.

On the other side of the clearing the trees weren't pines anymore. The branches all came together, and Tanya went astray inside the woods. She found herself in a maze of birches, but she knew she didn't have far to go. In the sky above the branches, a column of smoke caught the colors of the dawn.

Soon she could smell the smoke. She headed straight for it, over the yellow carpet of birch leaves.

The birches ended, and in front of Tanya were the

duck pond and the elm and her swing hanging down. She saw the well and the woodpiles, the orchard and the curve of the hill and the black pines high above it, and the dark mountains in the east with the sky shining behind them. She saw the stone walls of her house and barn. The smoke rose toward the last stars like the clouds in her dream of heaven.

In a hoarse voice she began calling for Milenka.

CHAPTER
THIRTY-ONE

Now that it was getting light, the villagers were looking once more for Mother Anna's little boy. Some had gone to the far corners of the farm. Others had divided up and were searching in the corn and wheat. The morning air carried Tanya's voice, and the villagers in the field heard her calling for her cow. They turned their heads and didn't believe their eyes.

She'd been through the flames, but not in the way the story was told, the story they told in the village for years afterward, about the girl whom the fire could not destroy. No one could explain it, though they talked about it enough. They went over it a thousand times. They said the Muffin Child had vanished in the middle of the night, that night of the Gypsies. Then the fire broke out in the barn. Her cow was in there, penned up, and she must have gone in to save it, she was so attached to that cow. Everyone thought she'd died in the fire, trying to save her cow; until they saw her the next morning. Many people saw her. She looked different. She was black with soot, her hair was all but burned away, her clothes were ragged and scorched. But it was Tanya.

Not everyone saw quite the same thing. Some said she emerged from the barn like a ghost haunting the place of its death. Others said she came out of thin air; they'd had their eyes on that patch of grass and suddenly, there she was. Most marvelous of all, five people swore they saw her walk right out of her house, with her hair on fire and a halo of crackling sparks; nothing, nothing could have lived through that blaze, they said; the heat had melted the cast iron of the oven, and there were pools of metal at its feet.

And then—even as they saw Tanya—then came the moment of almost unbearable relief, when down in the old barn at the bottom of the farm, they found Nikola. He was curled up in a stall, sound asleep; not a hair of his head had been harmed. Those toys he used to play with, those alphabet blocks (though they were more like cracked wooden apples from his endless handling)—they were lying beside him in the dust. The dust was thick with wool, and the oldest people in the village had something to say about that. They remembered a shepherd, Lupka was his name, he was a little soft in the head, and he used to put his sheep in there at night because he had no home and the barn was an abandoned place. But that was ages ago. No one had used it since.

No one, that is, except the Sharpener. They found his black picnic: his bread, sausage, a jug of brandy. In the dirt and dust they found the imprints of boots, a Gypsy's boots, with pointed toes and narrow heels. And in another part of the barn, where the harrows were stacked and the blades were as many as the teeth of a comb, they found Anton.

The men told the women to stay away, it wasn't a pretty sight. Mother Anna demanded to see him, she had a right to see the man who'd kidnapped her child. She was a woman never at a loss for words, Mother Anna; but when she came back out, she said nothing. Her eyes, bloodshot from the anxious night, were very wide, and they said what everyone was thinking. That justice had been done. And an injustice had been done.

They went away from that evil place. Mother Anna had such dignity about her as she carried her sleeping son in her arms. Pavel, who used to complain so about the little boy, his silence and his blocks—Pavel broke down. They joined the others who were gathered around Tanya, and Pavel fell to his knees, kissed the blocks in his hands, and cried.

"It was the Sharpener, Tanya," one of the others said.

"The Sharpener all along."

"How were we to know?"

"Please don't be angry with us."

Tanya seemed not to hear them. She went on calling for her cow.

"The blessed child lived through the fire."

"God has spared our children this morning."

"It's a miracle, a miracle, a miracle."

"Tanya, forgive us," a woman said, and knelt before her. The men took off their hats. Another woman said:

"Anna. Anna dear. Bring Nikola to her. Let her put her hand on the boy. Her touch will make him well."

But no one dared come near Tanya, nor did they stand in her way when she walked into the field of corn, calling her cow's name.

Everyone heard a crow, a single loud crow, and they looked to the treetops to see it on a bare branch, ruffling and shaking its wings.

"Where is she?" someone said. "Where'd she go?"

No one ever found her. The men went running through the cornstalks, all the way across the field to the edge of the woods, where the crow was croaking and clucking over their heads. Some ran on into the trees, and came back in a panic saying there were Gypsies on horses, that the woods were full of Gypsies. But they must have been seeing things, because no Gypsy showed his face.

Before the sun went down on that day, they got rid

of the Sharpener. They buried him inside the old barn and set fire to it. The mortar of the walls was rotten, and it wasn't hard for a team of men to topple the walls, sealing the ashes with stones.

Pavel started going around that winter saying the farm belonged to him now, he should have it, after all his family had been through. The more he said so, the less anyone challenged him. He went to work in the spring. He was smart about it. The whole farm was a shambles, but Pavel tended only the wheat. The next summer the wheat grew thick as hair on a newborn's head, and with the harvest money, Pavel hired help to replace the timbers and thatch on Tanya's barn. He did the same with the house, which became a second barn. Hard work and a few seasons did the rest. The farm was a glory again. Even the scorching on the stones of the barns was all on the inside.

Things went back to the way they were, the way they had always been. The villagers had the bridge repaired. They hired stonemasons from the seacoast to tear away the masts of the cypresses and the planks across the gorge and make the bridge firm again with the granite of the land. Anton's old mother passed away, the last and only guardian of his memory. The old woman talked nonsense to the end, saying Anton had just borrowed the little boy for a few hours, and if people wanted to point fingers, they should go to the mirror first. Mothers will say anything to protect their sons.

Nikola changed, a little for the better. He didn't need his blocks anymore. But the sight of cows in a meadow would upset him, and he would look around as if for some missing cow, the one that would make the herd complete.

He grew up, and watched over the cows on his father's farm. Children in the village were sometimes frightened of the strange man who slept on a bed of hay inside the big barn on the farm across the river. They were told that he was Nikola the Cowherd and he would never hurt anyone, he was different from other people, and in his whole life, no one had heard him speak.

CHAPTER
THIRTY-TWO

What happened to Tanya?"
For a week of nights, the mother sat on the bed and told the story, and each night the Tanya listening put her own face on the girl in the story, just as her mother had asked her to do. On the last night she saw herself with her hair burned off and her clothes in tatters. She saw herself wandering through the birches to the farm, and then the villagers gathering around her. But when the girl slipped behind the cornstalks, she lost sight of her.

"What happened to Tanya?" her mother said. "She went into the woods looking for Milenka, and she saw Gypsies. She was afraid, and she began to run. The trees went by like the spokes of a wagon wheel. She heard the horses stepping through the woods. She ran, but her legs seemed to be stuck in mud. She fell to the ground, and the last things she remembered were leaves and acorns, and the smell of earth.

"And then she was in a Gypsy wagon again, it was rolling, and she had a fever. The old woman with the long braids was with her, nursing her. She bandaged Tanya's arm where it had been burned in the fire. She rubbed Tanya's legs with steaming rags that smelled of vinegar. She lifted Tanya's head to help her drink a hot broth. It was so much like what Anton had said, about the Gypsies stealing children and giving them a broth that made them forget their own names; but Tanya wasn't afraid, because she knew that the Gypsies had saved her.

"The old woman tried other things, other cures, Gypsy cures. She made a blood-red tea with the skins of red berries floating in it. She held twigs with bitter-smelling leaves on them, and she dragged the leaves over Tanya's bare skin from her throat to her belly. And once, Tanya awoke to see her bare chest covered with little glass bells. The old woman held a burning candle inside each bell to warm the air inside, and then put it on Tanya's chest, where the heat made it stick. There seemed to be thousands of the little bells. But that was the fever.

"The fever lasted many days. The wagon shook, rocking Tanya as in a cradle. It was snowing outside, while she dreamed of a hot yellow sun over a wheat-field. The wheat swarmed with grasshoppers scratching and clicking their legs. The windowpane of the wagon was gray with snow, and there were grasshoppers crawling in the snow.

"When the fever broke, the grasshoppers flew away, and Tanya could think straight again. She wanted to go back and look for Milenka, but she was still too weak, and she had nowhere to go but with the Gypsies, like a leaf in the wind. She knew the old woman would never harm her. But Tanya was still afraid of her, only in a different way. She thought the old woman could read her mind. She was afraid of the old woman's eyes. They were gray eyes, almost the color of milk, and Tanya knew that if they *could* read her mind, then they could see the villagers in the night with their torches, and Mother Anna shaking Tanya, and Tanya saying: 'I saw them! I saw them take Nikola!'

"Tanya once asked the old woman: 'Why did you save me?' And the old woman answered: 'Because you are a child.' She never blamed Tanya for what happened that night on the farm. She said it was wrong to blame a child for the things grownups do.

"But Tanya always felt responsible. Remember what Anton said in the old barn, about people, and how they forget the bad things they've done? Just because it's easier not to remember? Tanya wasn't like that. She never forgot it. She never even tried to forget it. She couldn't. She told me she was never a child again, after that night."

"What do you mean, she told you?"

"I put something under your bed tonight. Did you see it?"

"No."

"Reach down and take a look."

It was a little box, like a jewelry box, with roses and stars all over it. The roses were made of sandalwood and cedar, the stars of mother-of-pearl. Tanya held the box in her hands. She felt the square edges against her palms. On one side some of the roses and stars were missing, and some were black. The fire in the barn.

"How did it get here?"

"Open it," her mother said.

The box didn't want to open at first. The lid was stuck. Then, with a soft clatter, the lid came off. Inside lay a photograph.

Old, very old; black and white and brown. Seven people were sitting and standing together to have their picture taken. You could see the planks of the floor under their feet, and the shapes of painted clouds behind them. There were three children—two girls and a boy—in the front row. A tall girl with bright eyes stood in back, with two men wearing crumpled fedora hats. One of the men held a beautiful old guitar, and under the wings of his moustache you could see the curl of a smile. And seated in front was the head of the family, an old woman whose braids ran down to her lap. She wore a long flowered skirt.

"Her name was Baba Zorina," Tanya's mother said. "Can you tell which one is Tanya?"

Tanya studied the faces, the eyes. She didn't want to be wrong. Her own eyes kept going to the girl in the back. The girl didn't look like someone in an old picture.

"That's Tanya!"

"No, her name was Mirza. Mirza was the Gypsy girl on the horse when Tanya ran from the old barn."

"Where's Tanya?"

Her mother pointed to the girl standing in front of Mirza. Long neck, round cheeks, round eyes. Her thick dark hair was cut in bangs, and her long braid hung like a rope beside the front buttons of her sweater.

"Your great-grandmother. She died before you were born." Her mother turned the picture to show the stamp on the back.

AURORA PHOTOGRAPHIC STUDIOS,
NEW YORK CITY.

And *1914,* scribbled with a pen.

"They came on a ship with black smoke pouring out of a smokestack, and two masts full of sails. She does look like you, doesn't she? I knew her when she was very old. She was our Baba Tanya, and she told all the grandchildren the story I've just told you; and when the story was told, we asked her to make muffins for us. She didn't want to at first. She said she was tired from telling the story. But she said all right, if we helped her.

"She sat in the kitchen, fingering her cane, and we gathered everything she told us to gather, the pans and the mixing bowl and flour and eggs and butter and milk and all the other things. We mixed the batter and put the pans in the oven, and we sat and stared at the oven. And as we smelled the muffins cooking, she began to speak about the old country, and how beautiful it was. How in the winter, when the sun was shining on the snow, the sky was such a deep blue it was almost like night. On summer nights when it was hot and she couldn't sleep, she would listen hard to the crickets, because they sounded like sleigh bells, like winter. And just listening to them cooled her off and she could sleep. And in the morning after she milked Milenka, she carried a pail full of milk across the barnyard, and she would see the bright yellow sunrise, like a baby chick hatching.

"So we listened to our Baba Tanya as she talked; and she said, 'The muffins are ready. Be careful now, the pan is hot. Be careful not to burn yourselves.' The muffins were so good, and we told her. She said, very quietly, 'They always said so.' "

Tanya's mother got up from the bed. The light went on at the end of the hall, and she opened the door of the closet where the towels and linens were kept. Tanya heard a whisper of paper. The hall light went out, and her mother returned.

She returned with something wrapped in faded old pink paper, the kind of paper you bunched up and stuffed inside a hat to keep its shape.

"Something for you."

Tanya took the paper off. It was a stuffed animal covered with patchwork: the stitching was broken in places, and you could see the yellow stuffing inside. The patchwork had been black and white once, and now it was shades of gray. The animal had four legs and a big head, and on the head there were two bulges, like horns.

A cow. A black-and-white spotted cow.

"This was your great-grandmother's. She made it herself, after she crossed the sea."

Tanya put it up to her nose.

"It's old," her mother said.

"I want to keep it."

In the middle of the night the cow got out from under the covers. Tanya brought her back in. Milenka smelled like stale chocolate, or like a dog just in from the rain.

Later, Milenka smelled like herself, like Milenka. The sun rose in the dark and burned behind the insects floating over the meadow. Tanya looked for the Muffin Child but didn't see her. The grass rustled at her feet, and she could feel Milenka's hide under the palm of her hand.